Dear Reader:

What if married couples decided to give each other a free Friday once a month to do whatever they want? Follow Leela and Riley, whose best friends, Bill and Samantha, become newly single and encourage them to join them on the social scene at bars and parties. Eventually, Riley suggests he and his wife try an innovative approach to saving their marriage. Although it's his idea, some surprising uncertainty comes along with the experiment.

Discover what happens in this thought-provoking read where relationships intertwine; some are new hookups and others are reconnections—for better or worse. In addition to her marital woes, Leela finds herself in the middle of family drama, including a stunning secret in her grandparents' marriage and its troubling effect on her mother, Linda, who struggles to cope once the revelation comes to light.

As always, thanks for supporting myself and the Strebor Books family. We strive to bring you the most cutting-edge, out-of-the-box material on the market. You can find me on Facebook @AuthorZane or you can email me at zane@eroticanoir.com.

Blessings,

Zane

Publisher
Strebor Books
www.simonandschuster.com

ALSO BY PAT TUCKER

Somebody Has to Pay

The Cocktail Club

Sideline Scandals

Party Girl

Daddy's Maybe

Lachez (an original e-book)

Football Widows

Daddy By Default

BOOKS WRITTEN WITH EARL SEWELL

Loyalty Among Friends

A Social Affair

Zane Presents

FREE FRIDAYS

PAT TUCKER

STREBOR BOOKS
NEW YORK LONDON TORONTO SYDNEY

Strebor Books
P.O. Box 6505
Largo, MD 20792
http://www.streborbooks.com

This book is a work of fiction. Names, characters, places and incidents are products of the author's imagination or are used fictitiously. Any resemblance to actual events or locales or persons, living or dead, is entirely coincidental.

ISBN 978-1-59309-590-1
ISBN 978-1-4767-7576-0 (e-book)
LCCN 2015957697

First Strebor Books trade paperback edition July 2016

Cover design: www.mariondesigns.com
Cover photograph: © Keith Saunders/Keith Saunders Photos

10 9 8 7 6 5 4 3 2 1

Manufactured in the United States of America

ACKNOWLEDGMENTS

I thank God for the endless blessings bestowed upon me. All of the love I can muster up to my patient and wonderful mother, Deborah Tucker Bodden; and the very best sister anyone could ever have, Denise Braxton; my handsome, loving husband, Coach Wilson, and the rest of my entire family. It is a challenging time in publishing so I wanted to give incredible high praise to ________________ (your name goes here!!!) Yes, you, the reader! I know now more than ever before you are bombarded with choices and that's what makes your selection of my work such a humbling experience. I will never take your support for granted and I vow to keep writing great, jaw-dropping stories for your reading pleasure. If I have forgotten anyone, and I'm sure I have, please be sure to charge it to my head and not my heart. Please be sure to connect with me on social media:

Pat Tucker

Authorpattucker

authorpattucker

Always feel free to drop me an email at pattuckerbooks@gmail.com.

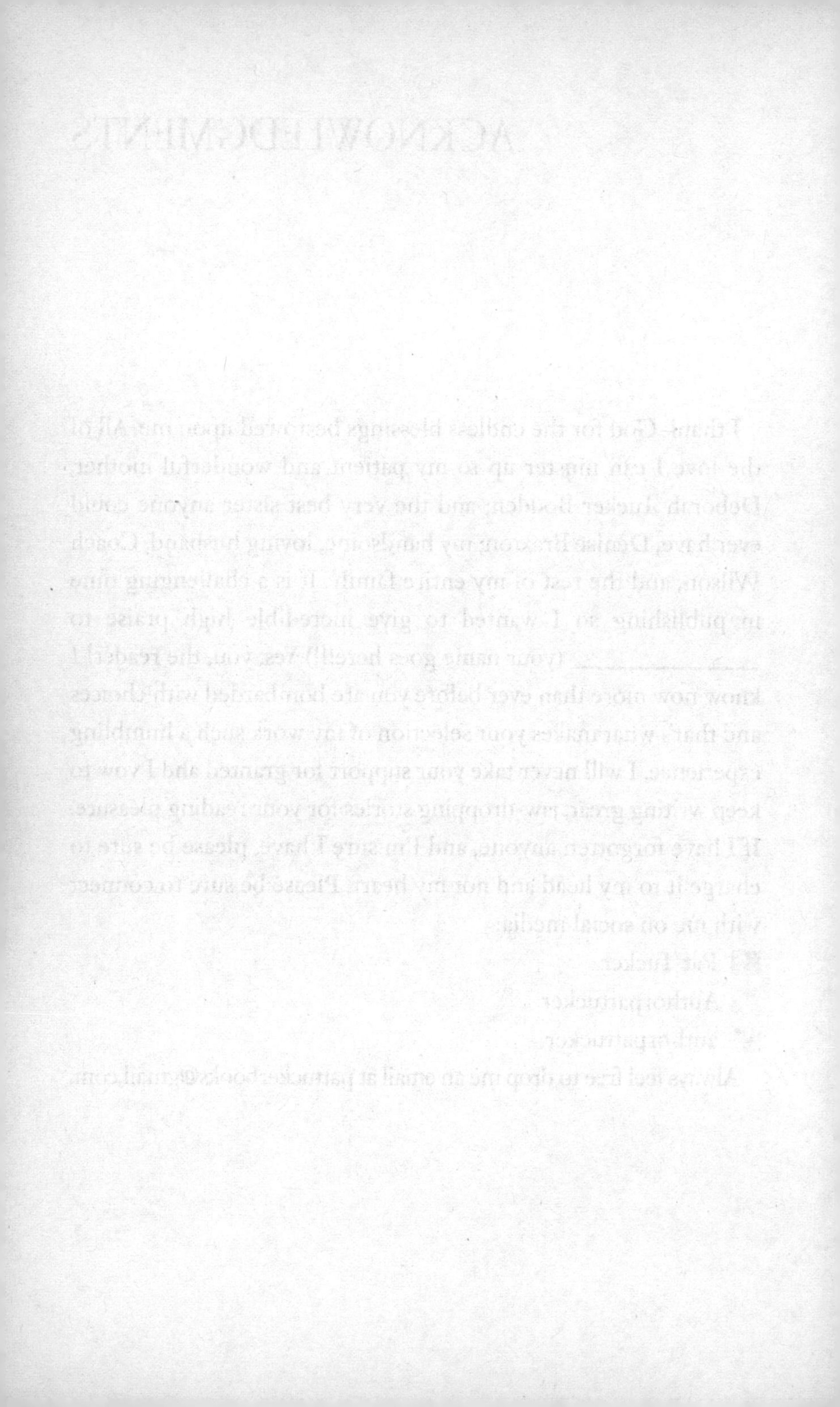

PROLOGUE

"What the hell?!" a stunned voice exclaimed.

Expensive champagne sprayed from Leela Franklin's perfectly painted lips as her eyes widened in stunned disbelief. Her mouth fell open and she struggled to believe what she saw.

"Jeeee-sus!" someone shrieked.

The Waterford crystal flute slipped from Leela's fingers and broke into pieces as it hit the marble floor. Two people jumped out of the way; droplets flew in every direction.

"OhMyGod!"

Leela's heart pounded against her chest. She looked around anxiously. Where was her best friend, Samantha Thomas? Better yet, where was her husband, Riley?

Every eye in the room was glued to the screen; the mouths of many people hung to the floor.

"Umph, umph, umph. Ain't that Samantha's husband, Bill?" Linda, Leela's mother, leaned closer and asked. "Chile, what kind of Mickey Fickey foolishness are these folks into?"

The dimmed lights that blanketed the room made it nearly impossible for Leela to make out where Samantha stood.

Had she planned this?

Why do it in front of an entire house full of friends, family, and co-workers?

Leela was embarrassed for her friend.

Minutes earlier, Samantha said she needed go get something from her bedroom and vanished. That was when the *anniversary video* started. Leela never thought much of Samantha's abrupt disappearance at such a crucial time. She figured Samantha had gone to find her husband. Wouldn't the happy couple want to be near each other while the video played?

But Bill had been across the room talking to Leela's husband, Riley, and a few of their colleagues.

Bill and Samantha Thomas were Leela and Riley's closest friends. Plans for their tenth anniversary party had been in the works for the past two months. Leela and Samantha had painstakingly gone over every detail. The video was supposed to set the tone for the evening and put everyone in a festive, celebratory mood. It was supposed to be a compilation of pictures that chronicled Bill and Samantha's life together.

Instead, it looked more like a raunchy, homemade, sex tape. The couple on it seemed to hump each other vigorously, on furniture, on the floor, and several times, in various showers. Their different outfits indicated that all the screwing had occurred over a period of time.

It was obvious that the video was recorded in secret, because it looked grainy, and from an angle that implied the camera was too far away to get the clear, crisp images most could appreciate.

Unfortunately for Bill, even with it being shot from a distance, the image of him and the woman who was not his wife was clear. This was despite the fact that some shots looked like they were blocked by furniture and even curtains.

Soon, gasps and whispers rose from the crowd gathered in the room. Noises and chatter grew louder as the shocking images continued to play out on the seventy-inch flat-screen. The size of the screen made their explicit acts appear larger than life.

"I need to find Sam!" exclaimed Leela.

She looked around, and cautiously stepped over the liquid and shattered glass at her feet, and went in search of Samantha. But a sudden rush of brightness stopped Leela cold. She looked up and saw Samantha perched on the second-floor landing, looking down at the crowd.

The expression on her face was not one of horror or devastation like Leela expected to see.

How could she appear so calm and collected while all of this was going on? People in the room were seconds away from flying into a frenzy, and Samantha was upstairs, seemingly coasting above it all.

"That's just a glimpse of the steamy love affair that's been going on between my husband and his tramp at the office," Samantha said. Her voice was just as calm as her demeanor.

Samantha wore her fancy sequined dress, but was barefoot, and her hair looked like she'd been on the losing end of a tussle. Leela struggled to get a handle on the situation. When had things spiraled so out of control? Earlier, Samantha seemed fine, didn't she?

"You nasty, cheating bastard!" Samantha finally screamed. She pointed a crooked finger in Bill's direction.

All eyes found, and zeroed in on Bill.

Bill appeared nervous under the glare of the sudden attention. The color seemed to seep from his face and perspiration settled on his forehead. He was fidgety and he wore a guilty expression.

"Samantha! Stop this shit right the hell now!"

"You don't tell me what the hell to do! I'm not Kelly! Go tell Kelly what to do! All of the lies and deception. You are one sick, cheating, low-life bastard!"

Riley looked back and forth between the two, as did almost everyone in the room.

Bill made a move toward the staircase, but Riley stepped in and blocked his path.

"Not a good move, Dawg. You're too mad right now," Riley said.

Bill's nostrils flared; rage flashed in his eyes. He looked at his friend, then up at his wife, as he balled and unballed his fists. "Samantha, this is completely uncalled for!"

"Oh, I'm just getting started!" Samantha spat. "You wait 'til I'm done with your no-good ass!"

The video still played while they fussed at each other.

Leela's body stiffened. Her eyes were touched with alarm as she glanced around the crowded room. She wasn't sure what she should do.

All of a sudden, a loud clapping noise sounded, and Linda's voice rang out. That seemed to pull people's attention away from the video and the argument.

"Okay, folks, this party is over! Please, start making your way to the front door." Linda walked toward the TV, and snatched a plug from the outlet. Her knack for taking control came in handy because Leela had been frozen into inaction by the series of events and how everything had played out.

The screen finally went black.

Leela looked at her mother and mouthed the words, "Thank you," as she moved toward the stairs. She needed to talk some sense into Samantha.

People seemed reluctant to leave at first. But Linda walked around, removed glasses from hands, and reiterated that it was time to go.

"C'mon, please, see yourselves out," she said, as she motioned toward the front door. "C'mon, right this way; let's keep it moving."

Soon, Riley followed her lead, and urged the remaining guests to leave. Once the room was finally cleared, Bill seemed to get lost in the shuffle, because he was nowhere to be found.

The Monday afternoon following the anniversary party fiasco, things had gone from bad to worse quickly.

"Don't do nothing stupid, Dawg," Riley warned Bill over the phone. "She ain't worth a second in jail. Believe that, Man!" He sighed. "I know you pissed, and you have every right to be, but try to calm down, Dawg."

This was the kind of shit Riley himself would never put up with. He wore the pants in his house and not a day went by that he didn't let it be known. His buddy Bill was cut from a completely different cloth. Riley felt that Bill allowed his wife to do as she pleased; she dressed any kind of way, and she was far too loud and too damn outspoken. It was no wonder they were in the mess they were in.

But as a good friend, Riley knew he couldn't point those shortcomings out at that moment. His goal now was to try and keep his friend and co-worker out of jail.

"I could kill her, Man," Bill said. His hands gripped the steering wheel so tightly, his knuckles changed colors. "I could lose it all. Everything, Man," he said. Spittle gathered at the corners of Bill's mouth as he pushed the words out angrily.

Riley could feel his pain, but still, he would never be caught up in anything like this. It wasn't just that Bill was a Beta Male; of course that played a role, but Riley felt Bill was just too soft when it came to managing his household.

Riley knew women behaved like they wanted equality, but when it came down to it, all women wanted a man who could put them in their place. They'd never widely admit it because they didn't want to be attacked by feminists, but Riley knew deep down, that was just about every woman's true desire. Riley was the epitome of an Alpha Male.

And Leela was perfect for him because she didn't make much of a fuss about anything. Even when she had her moments, she knew better than to act out the way Samantha had at that party. Oh no, that would never happen under Riley's watch.

"Aey, Bill?" Riley called into the phone again.

Bill's Hummer screeched to a stop in the circular driveway as he pulled up in front of the house.

"Look, I just made it here, Man. I'ma holler at you later," Bill huffed. Adrenaline raced through his veins like a NASCAR competitor.

"Bill. Remember what I said, Dawg. Just chill. Don't do nothing stupid."

If he were in Bill's shoes, this might be the one time he broke his own cardinal rule: never lay hands on a female. Riley didn't want to see his boy go to jail for domestic violence, but this time, Samantha had it coming after all she had done.

"I hear you, Bruh. I hear ya'," Bill said.

He ended the call, barely cut off the ignition, threw his Hummer into park, and hopped out. His heart raced at an uncontrollable rate as he rushed up the three steps in one leap and pulled open the massive, cast-iron and smoked glass double doors. Bill was breathing like a bull when he stormed through the front door and stopped at the foyer.

"Samantha! What the hell? You put that crap on Facebook?!" he yelled as he stepped inside.

His thunderous baritone was filled with rage as it echoed and bounced off the vaulted ceiling and brightly colored walls. With wild, desperate eyes, he searched the room for his wife, then headed to the spiral staircase when he didn't see her.

"Samantha! I know you're here! What the hell were you thinking?!" he yelled up toward the second level of their lavish home. Spittle fanned out in every direction as he fired off his words.

Moments later, Samantha strutted into view. Satisfaction was written all over her face. "I told you Saturday night that I was just getting started. I guess you thought sneaking outta here, like the true punk you are, was gonna somehow make this all go away. Umph! I knew you was screwing that tramp! I just knew it; I felt it in my gut! Can't deny it now, can you?!" she yelled back from upstairs.

The smirk on her face was unapologetic. With her arms spread on both sides, she swiveled her neck as she leaned over the banister and taunted Bill even more.

"You nasty, cheating dog! Now the whole world knows what a sleaze you are!" Samantha's voice was thick with hatred. She twisted her face and looked down at him with a menacing glare.

Rage tore through every fiber in Bill's body as he looked up at her. He was ready to kill.

His cell phone rang and he considered ignoring the call, but figured he couldn't. Clients had been calling nonstop since the posts went live. With his eyes still glued to his wife, he snatched the phone from his waist, then pulled it up to focus on the screen. It was his boss, Gary Watson. He had to decompress and pull himself together—quickly.

Gary Watson was a grumpy old man who ruled his family-owned finance firm with a hawk-like eye that rarely missed a thing.

"Hello?" Bill struggled to calm himself. He had to handle Gary just right.

"Bill. We're all very concerned about these social media postings," Gary said.

"Yes, Mister Watson. This is all just a big misunderstanding. Kelly and I are—"

"The board has decided to launch an investigation," Gary said firmly, cutting Bill off. "We're placing you on leave pending the outcome."

"Yes, Sir," Bill said.

Bill's heart thudded so loudly, he feared his boss would hear it through the phone. It had been bad enough that a house full of people saw the video, but now, with everything prominently on display for the world to see on social media, Bill felt he had no leg to stand on. He'd have to get an attorney to help clean up this mess and hopefully save his job.

"We're in the business of protecting our clients' assets. How does it look to have your inappropriate personal business spread across social media for everyone to see? It's very unprofessional, not to mention irresponsible. We've talked with Ms. Anderson as well. There is a morality clause in your contracts," he said.

Ms. Anderson was Kelly Anderson, Bill's coworker, and mistress. Bill palmed his forehead as he listened to his boss. But his mind raced with the many ways he could possibly kill his wife with his bare hands.

She had gone too far this time. Seven-figure jobs didn't come along often.

With his eyes closed, he was instantly transported to that moment, nearly two hours earlier, when he was in his office at work. Riley had called and dropped the bombshell.

"Dude. I see you and Sam still at it. I know she's pissed, but damn, Dawg, why she call you out like that, and on Facebook too?"

"What you talking about, Playboy?" Bill had asked coolly. He didn't like the sound of Riley's question. He hated social media sites and used them only for business and networking purposes.

"Oh, snap! You ain't seen that shit yet?!" Riley yelled. "See, this is why you need to have more control over your woman and what she does."

Bill's features fell into a concentrated frown.

"I wish Leela would show her ass like that, Man," Riley added.

As he talked, Bill used trembling fingers, and pulled up his Facebook page.

"Shiiit. That's what's wrong with women; they make emotional moves and screw it up for everybody," Riley said.

Heat crawled up Bill's shoulders and slithered up his neck to his hairline, as his mind conjured up all sorts of thoughts. He had avoided home since Samantha pulled her stunt Saturday night. Bill thought it was best he stay away to try and give things a chance to calm down.

"Oh, I'd tap that ass for sure," Riley continued.

The moment Bill's eyes connected with the images, and the lewd descriptions beneath each one, he began to hyperventilate.

"Wwh-hat the fu—"

"That's what I said," Riley commented. "Dawg, that video was enough. Besides, how she get all that on you? I told you about being sloppy, Man."

Bill wanted to cry like a newborn denied food. His Facebook account was designed to share finance-related news with his clients. His bosses insisted they needed to be active and visible on all social media platforms. Bill was reluctant, but fell in line after Samantha agreed to manage the pages for him. He knew very little about social media and never cared to learn. Now, that decision had come back to bite him in the butt.

"Let me guess, you probably don't know the first thing about pulling that mess down, huh?" Riley said.

"She handles all of that; I just pulled up the page and of course all this crap is right here for anyone to see."

"Damn, that means she has your settings on public."

Bill shook that disastrous thought from his head. He needed to deal with the current crisis that threatened to ruin him both professionally and financially. When his boss finished reciting clauses in the contract, he wanted to wrap up the call so he could deal with Samantha's evil behind.

"This is very concerning," Mr. Watson repeated.

"Okay, Mr. Watson. I understand and I appreciate the call. I assure you, I'm going to straighten this thing out right away," Bill said. His voice lacked the usual confidence that he'd been known to possess in the past.

No sooner had he ended the call, than pieces of his clothing came falling down like thick raindrops from the second floor.

"Go back and stay with Kelly, since you two can't seem to keep your hands off each other!" Samantha yelled as she tossed boxer briefs, neckties, and slacks over the banister.

"Are you crazy? I may have lost my damn job behind your dumb ass!" Bill yelled. "If I lose my job, Samantha—"

"You oughta be glad you didn't lose your damn life!"

"After the stunt you pulled at the party, you posted that mess on Facebook? You need to remove that crap now! What the hell, Samantha?! I was trying to give you some time to calm down. All you had to do was call me," he said.

"Call you! Why? So you could lie and weasel your way out of it? Oh, no. I think posting the hotel receipts, pictures of you and your cheating tramp sneaking into the room, and copies of your sleazy emails for everyone to see was definitely the right move." Samantha tossed a few pairs of shoes over the banister.

"Oh. And I ain't removing a damn thing!" She breathed heavily as she mustered up the strength to toss even more of his items over the banister.

"Your ass don' gone ape-shit crazy for real!" Bill said.

"Get out! Get the hell out! I'm tired and I want you gone!" Samantha screamed. "Go back to wherever you were and don't bother coming back here!"

From Bill's vantage point, his wife looked like a madwoman. Her weave was strewn all over her head, wild and untamable. Her face was streaked with traces of dried makeup and she wore nothing but a slip dress.

They'd been having major problems from the moment Samantha found out he and Kelly were working together a year and a half ago. Bill had done everything he could to convince his wife that there was nothing going on between him and the sexy vixen.

And at first, there wasn't. But his wife's constant nagging, and a sudden burst of attention from Kelly herself, had led to his current situation.

That, and the fact that Kelly Anderson was too much for Bill to resist. Kelly didn't walk; she sashayed in all her designer-clad glory. Her tight skirts, eye-catching blouses, and her pouty lips that formed a perfect "O," when she was amused, only added to her mystique. Her false lashes, glossy lips, and dangerous curves left him weak; he fell for her hard. He thought he was being careful, had covered his tracks, and taken all of the necessary precautions, but it was obvious he hadn't; they hadn't.

"Get the fuck out!" Samantha yelled.

Before he could agree, bottles of after-shave, cologne, and shampoo came flying over the banister.

Bill used his arms to cover his head as he darted toward the corner for cover.

"You don' lost your mind!"

"Get the fuck out!" Samantha screamed.

"You're gonna regret this shit, Sam! Mark my words; my word is bond. I swear to you," Bill said.

CHAPTER 1

Leela had wiped the exact same spot on the granite countertop more times than she could count. For the better part of the evening, she'd been crying uncontrollably. She knew she needed to snap out of it. But despite her best efforts, her mind was overrun with thoughts of Samantha's life without Bill.

She felt odd knowing her best friend's husband had been cheating. What would become of Samantha now that Bill was gone?

"You still there?" Samantha asked.

"Sorry; yes, girl. Where's Bill?"

"I don't know and I don't give a damn! I'm sick of this game. I hope it was all worth it to him."

As Samantha went on about how she looked forward to being rid of her husband, Leela thought back to happier times. She and her husband double-dated with Samantha and Bill; they had gone on family cruises with Big Mama and Pah-pah; vacationed together; and for all Leela knew, all of their marriages were on solid ground. Well, at least hers and Big Mama's were.

Despite the failed anniversary party, Leela fought the strong urge to question all she thought she knew. Samantha seemed to be taking everything in stride and behaved as if her crumbled marriage was nothing but a mere bump in the road.

"I'm gonna do some things I'd been putting off because I felt trapped," Samantha said.

The comment brought Leela back to their conversation.

"Trapped? What do you mean by that?"

"Leela. Men act like a marriage license entitles them to ownership. Well, not all men. I mean, they just don't make them like your grandfather anymore. But all I'm saying is, for years, I avoided doing things that might cause conflict or problems with Bill and me. No more! I'm gonna do what the hell I want, when and where I want! It's that simple!"

"I never realized you felt so—"

"Well, I did." Samantha cut her off. "But that's all in the past. I'm so over the years I wasted with Bill. It's time for me to start my new and improved life! That trifling bastard did me a favor; I just didn't know it at the time."

"Sam. You sure you're gonna be okay?"

Leela thought maybe her friend was experiencing shock. Reality would hit when Samantha least expected it and she'd be devastated by the loss of her husband.

"Am I gonna be okay? Why wouldn't I be? Leela. Look, it's like I said; I knew something was going on. I may not have been able to verbalize what it was, but why do you think I hired that private investigator? I'm nobody's fool. I saw the little clues here and there, but I also knew I had to play my cards right."

"I don't know what to say," Leela said.

"Honey, there's nothing for you to say. I told you, I had a feeling something was going on. I just needed concrete evidence."

Leela was experiencing a series of emotions that she couldn't understand nor explain. She seemed more devastated by the breakup than Samantha. She knew that wasn't the case, but Samantha was very nonchalant about what had happened.

Conversations about the Thomases' marriage only happened when Leela initiated it. Although she didn't want to make her friend feel bad, Leela couldn't wrap her mind around the fact that the end of a marriage seemed to represent a new and exciting beginning for Sam.

Leela thought she would need to be near the phone to offer moral and emotional support, but those calls never came. Over the past few days, if she hadn't reached out to Samantha, Leela wouldn't have heard from her.

Although Leela had a problem with that, the current conversation made her feel like there was no point in bringing that up.

"And you know what?" Samantha asked.

Leela didn't respond.

"I hope they both get fired!"

"You want them to lose their jobs?"

"Why not? They didn't care about those jobs when they snuck away from the office for their little rendezvous. Why should they be able to keep them?"

For Leela, the conversation was becoming exhausting. Samantha was hurt, but it was also clear she was hell-bent on seeing Bill suffer.

"Leela, you work in HR. What would you do if you found out that two married senior executives were having an affair?"

Before Leela could answer, Samantha blurted out a response.

"Their asses would be canned! You don't have to admit it. It's not a good look, not in the office, not among the clients. It's not, and you know it. Those two knew it too, but they didn't care."

Leela listened as Samantha carried on about all of the bad and painful things she prayed would happen to Bill.

Bouts of depression seemed to stick to Leela like a bad shadow that wouldn't go away. She'd go to work, go through the motions, then go home and prepare to do it all again. She did all of this as she struggled to hide her emotional roller coaster from Riley because she knew his tolerance level was very low when it came to what he called her mood swings.

One weekend morning, Riley walked into the room and didn't speak.

His presence made Leela feel awkward. But she told herself there was nothing wrong with being in her bed in mid-afternoon. She had nearly convinced herself that it was okay, until Riley spoke.

"You getting outta bed today, or what?"

"What's that supposed to mean?"

Leela knew what he meant, but she wanted to hear his answer.

"Yeah, okay, Leela," was all he said.

"Oh, and to answer your question, I'm meeting Big Mama and my mother for a late lunch in a little while, so please don't hog all the hot water."

Several hours later, Leela talked to her mother on the phone as she drove. "I'm looking for the address, but I can't find it and I've been around the block three times already." Leela was frustrated as she searched for the restaurant where she was meeting her mother and grandmother for lunch.

"I'll walk outside," her mother said. "Give me a few seconds. I'm gonna stay on the phone with you."

Linda Bishop walked out of the restaurant to look for her daughter. A frown lived on her face, even when she wasn't angry. Her dark-brown eyes matched her features and her attitude on most days.

Linda's was very outspoken regardless of the topic or issue. She was the bully of the family, and most of her relatives simply cowered in her presence because they didn't want to use the energy for a fight that was hard to win.

Leela kept the car in park as she looked around the West Chase strip mall. All of the buildings and storefronts looked the same, and it was hard to read addresses even when they were visible.

Suddenly, she saw a figure in the far distance waving an arm. It was her mother, Linda.

"Oh. I see you," she said. "I'm on the other end, but here I come."

Leela drove to the opposite end of the strip mall and pulled into a parking space. Her mother approached her car and gave her a tight hug the second she came out of the car.

"Now, listen. Your grandmother wants to tell you what happened in her own words. She begged me not to say anything because she felt like you needed to hear it from her and be told in person. But I need to warn you. This is gonna be hard to accept. And, it's gonna be almost impossible for you to look at your Pah-pah the same ever again."

A sinking feeling threatened to overwhelm Leela as she listened to her mother. Considering the mess between her best friend and her husband, she knew she wasn't ready for any more earth-shattering news. She especially didn't want to hear anything bad about her grandparents. Leela felt vulnerable; she simply couldn't handle any more.

"I don't like the sound of this," Leela admitted. "I don't want to hear any more bad news. I'm scared."

"Yes. I know. We all are. This is foreign to us all, but I think once you hear her side of the story, you'll agree, she didn't have any other option," Linda said.

"What do you mean she didn't have any other option? Ohmy-God! What's going on? What is the world coming to? I don't think I'm ready for this," Leela whined.

Her mother stopped her abruptly.

"Leela. It's time for you to pull your grown woman panties up. This situation is real and it's going to change all of our lives. Your grandmother needs your support right now. This is not a time to be emotional; she needs us all to be strong. I know you're probably still messed up over that situation with Samantha and Bill, but you need to pull it together!"

"I know, but—"

"There are no buts." Linda cut her off. "It is what it is. Let's get up there and get this over with because she's waiting on you."

Leela pulled herself together as best she could, pushed thoughts of Samantha and her own fears to the back of her mind. She followed her mother up the stairs to the little Mexican restaurant where her grandmother waited. Linda's incomplete explanation was the only preparation she'd received to deal with the kind of news that nobody should ever have to swallow.

CHAPTER 2

Startled by a strange sound, Riley flinched. It felt like his heart had been zapped with one of those defibrillators. His handsome features contorted into a frown as sudden shock gripped his heart. The most important muscle in his body felt like it had taken a nosedive from his ribcage to the soles of his feet. Beneath the shower's hot, jet-like rays, he glanced around the spacious en-suite bathroom.

"Ww-what that fu...?"

Where's the but? Is the nine-mil in the lockbox?

A twinge of adrenaline shot through him as he grasped the knob and cut off the water.

Riley pushed the smoked-glass door open and removed the thick, white, terrycloth bath sheet from a nearby hook. He stepped out of the shower, threw the towel around his washboard abs, and advanced across the floor. His house was more secure than the Pentagon, so he wasn't worried about an intruder, but he was concerned about his wife. She wasn't the most stable, but that was okay, because he couldn't deal with one of those so-called, strong-willed, independent women. He had grown to expect her mood swings, unexpected bouts of tears or blank stares.

"Leela?" he called out to his wife. She usually spoke up if she walked in after being gone. Lunch with her mother and grandmother ran kind of long. But he'd just returned from balling with the fellas, so it was all good.

When Riley heard Leela groan again, instead of answering, he rushed toward the noise. Flashes of the family room's sleek and contemporary décor mixed with the silk drapes, the chandelier, and area rugs, served as a backdrop for the most unusual sight.

Riley stopped abruptly at the vision before him: his wife sat on the ottoman with a look of bewilderment on her face. Riley couldn't help but wonder whether she'd been spooked by someone or something.

At the sight of her, he wondered whether she had gotten her period and was about to get all emotional. He hated that time of the month the most. It seemed like Leela was bipolar during that time, the ups and downs, the constant complaints about cramps. He hated it.

His eyes looked around their lavish home for anything that might be responsible for Leela's sudden torment. They had plans to go to a colleague's party after they both got home. He wondered if her mother or grandmother had told her about a fatal illness. Something had happened, and whatever it was, it had left his wife broken. Her shoulders were hunched in despair as she stared off blankly into space. Riley could tell she barely wanted to look up at him, but he had already heard her cries, the evidence that something had gone terribly wrong.

"Jesus! Leela, what's the matter?" he asked. "Did something happen when you were with your mom and Big Mama?"

When Leela finally looked up, her tear-stained face was lined with anguish. Her eyes were bloodshot, and it bothered Riley to see her in so much pain.

"Big Mama left my grandfather," she muttered, her tone filled with angst.

For a moment, Riley stood open-mouthed as he tried to make sense of the words she'd just said. It might as well have been a riddle, because his brain couldn't compute. His wife's grandparents, affectionately known as Big Mama and Pah-pah had been married for nearly fifty-two years. That was longer than he'd been alive.

Riley remembered how, on his very own wedding day six years ago, his late mother whispered that Leela had come from good stock. She referred to Leela's grandparents' marriage and told Riley to look at them for guidance on happily-ever-after. Riley's mother was a divorcee.

At a loss for words, he rubbed her back and tried to convince himself that there had to be a good reason for the separation. Maybe the old man got tired of his wife mouthing off all the time, or maybe Big Mama had forgotten her place in their household. The Bishops were headed for divorce? It simply couldn't be.

He'd never known anyone personally who'd been married more than fifteen years. What did his wife always say? The Bishops were an institution, at church, and at work. They had been the real-life symbol of black love. Obviously, that wasn't really the case.

Riley looked down at his wife and struggled for suitable words because he knew nothing in his vocabulary could fit the situation. He wanted to tell her to hold off until she got the whole story, but he didn't.

"What do you mean?" he managed.

"They're getting a divorce, selling the house, and…" She choked up before her voice trailed off. Her sniffles erupted into a full sob and Riley was frustrated.

He had lots of questions, but didn't have the patience to endure more crying if he asked them. Did Mr. Bishop cheat on his wife? Nah, that silver fox couldn't still have it in him, could he?

The sound of the ringing phone broke the eerie silence that had blanketed the family room. They both looked in its direction, but it was Riley who reached for the phone.

"Shit," he said. "The party," he added. "You know what, we don't have to go."

Leela looked up with a frown. "No. We've gotta go, Babe. We can't just not show up. That's your co-worker."

With all that was already going around the office about Bill and Kelly's affair, Riley knew his absence would be noticed, but if he couldn't make it, he couldn't.

"You sure?" Riley felt if he explained what had gone down, anyone would understand. Things like birthday and anniversary parties were really for females anyway.

"Go on; go finish getting ready," Leela said.

"I don't think you're in any condition to party," Riley said.

Before Riley could say anything else, Leela rose and strode across the room. "I'm okay, Babe. Gonna go shower," she said over her shoulder as she darted around the corner.

In the master bedroom, Leela tried to pull herself together before she returned a missed call from Samantha. Thoughts of Samantha, and now Big Mama's failed marriage, made her heart heavy.

Leela decided she'd try to forget about the news she'd just received. It would be a major challenge since she could barely swallow it herself. There was a part of her that never wanted to admit it to Riley, but there was no way she would've gotten away with keeping that unbelievable news to herself. Of course they should still go to the party.

She pressed a button on the phone and pulled it up to her ear. All sorts of thoughts ran through her mind as she waited for Samantha to answer.

"Hey, what's up?" Samantha greeted.

Samantha's voice sounded odd.

Leela brushed it off and told herself the entire world hadn't fallen off its axis because her grandparents were calling it quits after fifty-two years of marriage. It still didn't sound right, even when the words were just bouncing around in her head. What's a deal breaker after more than a half-century of marriage? She couldn't imagine.

"Sorry, Sam; what's going on?"

"What are you sorry about?"

"Oh, my bad. Girl, nothing. I'm just. My mind is all over the place. I'm...well, you know what, enough about me. What's up? How's everything going?"

It nearly killed Leela not to tell Samantha the devastating news.

CHAPTER 3

One of the hardest things Samantha had to do was answer the questions that seemed to flow nonstop since the anniversary party. She'd been working the phones to the best of her ability, but she knew she wouldn't be able to handle it much longer. Everyone expected her to be broken and near devastation. But she was the opposite. She was ready to move on.

Several days had passed since the last confrontation with Bill, and she still felt like she should've done more. Maybe she should've paid to have his car trashed, or burned his clothes.

For a long time, she had suspected something was going on, but there was still a part of her that wished she'd never found out. It wasn't that she'd had that false sense of security; she simply knew that life would get complicated if her husband refused to get rid of his long-term mistress. The longer he banged her, the more he ran the risk of falling in love with her.

To Samantha, an occasional piece of ass on the side was different from a woman who felt she was merely waiting in the wings. Everyone grew tired of waiting, and that's when they usually got desperate.

As she held the phone to her ear, she knew Leela was still there because she heard her breathe, but her friend was speechless.

"So what are you gonna do?" Leela finally asked after she listened to details of how Samantha's worst fears had been confirmed.

"Well, he's living in the guest house for now, but we're not gonna make it," Samantha admitted.

"Oh no," said Leela. "I'm so sorry to hear all of this."

"Leela, I did all of this in such a public way for a reason. There's no way in hell I want him back after everyone knows all about his little secret. I don't want him back and I don't want people feeling like there's hope for us."

"I hear what you're saying, but maybe you should take some time to really think this through. I'm not saying your decision isn't the right one; actually, I think I am. I mean, it's ten years, Samantha. Let's talk about this some more."

"We can talk about it all you want, but I've gotta be honest. You're wasting valuable breath. There's nothing more to discuss when it comes to Bill and me. I'm done!"

"You need to give it more time; that's all I'm saying. You know what? I'm coming over there." Leela didn't wait for Samantha to respond. "I'll be there in a few."

When Riley came out of their walk-in closet and found his wife sitting on the bed, not dressed, and again staring off, he struggled to maintain his patience. He wasn't in the mood for one of her emotional breakdowns.

"Leela, you don't look so good. Maybe we need to stay here tonight."

At the sound of his voice, Leela turned to see her handsome husband with a look of concern across his face. He wore a dark pair of designer jeans, a crisp white Oxford shirt, and a blazer. In his ensemble, Riley looked good enough to grace the cover of *GQ* magazine. And he smelled great.

"I—I feel so lost right now," Leela said.

Riley moved over to her side, and took her into his arms.

"Everything is falling apart. I don't know what's going on around us," Leela cried.

He didn't like when she was reduced to a pile of emotions, but he knew he had to be supportive.

"No, babe. It's not everything. I feel you. I can't imagine your grandparents without each other, but that doesn't mean everything is falling apart. I know you talked with Big Mama, but what about your grandpops? Have you talked to him yet?"

He didn't understand why men couldn't take control of their households. Leela's grandfather had held it down for fifty-two years! Riley couldn't imagine what had gone wrong and how he had lost control after such a long time. Even though he didn't want to hurt his wife's feelings, Riley felt like maybe there was a good reason the Bishops had decided to call it quits.

"No. My mom is with my grandmother, but when I try to ask about him, neither of them want to talk about it. But I wasn't talking about them this time. I'm talking about Bill and Sam," Leela said. "It's final. They're getting a divorce too."

Riley pulled back slightly. That's when it dawned on him that he hadn't heard from Bill since Thursday. Here it was Saturday evening, and he had no idea what had happened after Bill had gone home to confront Samantha. He had assumed no collect call from jail meant Bill had held it together. Hell, all the man had to do was go home and put his foot down.

"What do you mean they're getting a divorce? I just talked to Bill the other day, and told him what was what... I mean, he was all worked up, but..." Realizing he may have been saying too much, Riley looked at his wife and asked, "So they didn't make up? I meant to call him, but things got crazy at work yesterday."

"Make up? Riley, it's over between them!" Leela was dumbstruck by the suggestion. "As a matter-of-fact, I'm gonna go over there now. Sam really needs me," Leela said. "I was waiting to tell you."

"So this is it then?"

"Yeah, babe. She just told me. I called her while you were getting dressed. She sounds really bad. You don't mind, do you?"

"Nah, not at all. It's all good. I would've thought Bill would've called me or said something."

"Ry, who knows what's going on over there? Actually, you should probably come with me. Samantha said he moved into the guest house."

A surprised expression made its way to Riley's face.

Leela got up and moved across the room to the dresser. Now it was her turn to console her husband. Riley had taken her seat at the edge of the bed.

"I thought it was just her acting out again. Why did she put all their business out there like that? All over social media?" Riley said. "I know that's what she does, but damn, that was foul."

"What are you saying over there?" Leela asked.

Riley told her the story about the Facebook posts and how he had called to bring it to Bill's attention. As he described what he had seen to his wife, he also told her that he thought Bill would be within his legal rights if he would've slapped her up a bit.

That admission left Leela at a loss for words.

"So you knew about Bill's affair all this time? Is that what you're telling me?"

Riley didn't answer right away. A few seconds later, Leela looked him in the eyes and repeated the question.

"What's that gotta do with anything?"

Before Leela could say anything else, Riley rose and walked out of their bedroom.

That answered her question, even though he wouldn't.

Thirty minutes later, Leela called out to her husband. Finally showered, changed, and ready to go, she didn't feel better emotionally, but at least the shower had left her refreshed.

"Ry?!" she yelled.

Their home was a large, multilevel structure, with Riley's mancave on the lower level. When he didn't respond, Leela knew he must've been inside his oasis. She left the master suite, walked down the stairs, and passed through the family room.

"Hey, Riley, you ready?" she asked, as she approached the door to his area and eased it open.

Riley rose from one of the theater-style seats and straightened his jeans. He had replaced the button-down and blazer with a V-neck T-shirt.

"Yeah. I tried to call Bill, but all I got was voicemail," Riley said. His eyes settled on Leela and confusion colored his face.

"That's what you're wearing?"

"What's wrong with what I'm wearing?" Leela looked down at the outfit she had on. It was fine to her. She looked back up at her husband.

Riley gave her a stern look. "You're answering my question with a question, and you know how I feel about that. Now please, go put on something else. A pair of jeans and a T-shirt is more appropriate for this situation."

Leela looked down at the maxi dress again. She didn't see a problem with it, but just to avoid an argument, she decided to change. It would be easier than to listen to him go on about what was and wasn't appropriate attire to sit up at her friend's house.

"Okay, but I still think you should come with me," Leela said, as she turned to go back to their bedroom. What difference did it make whether she wore a dress or jeans? Sometimes, Riley could be so irrational, but she brushed it off and kept it moving.

"Better?" She met him in the family room and twirled to get his approval.

"Yeah, and I'll drive. If he's not there, I'll just drop you off," he offered.

"Thanks," Leela said, and they headed to the garage.

CHAPTER 4

Cross Creek Ranch, Fort Bend County's master-planned community, was a status symbol for anyone fortunate enough to call it home. Bill and Samantha Thomas's pristine, lakefront neighborhood looked like it should grace the pages of *Design Digest*. Their four-bedroom, two-story, stucco-and-brick house, near the back of Liberty Heights, was adjacent to one of the many neighborhood pocket parks. The area was serene and tranquil.

As their car slowly rolled along the winding cobblestone circular driveway, Leela couldn't help but wonder whether this would be one of their last trips to the picturesque gated-community.

"I'm gonna drop you here and pull around to the back," Riley said.

"Yeah. That's probably a good idea. I told you she didn't sound too good on the phone, so I don't want her to see you, especially since you might not stay anyway," Leela explained.

Riley pulled up beyond the front door and brought the car to a slow stop so his wife could get out.

"You want me to call when I'm ready?" she asked.

"Yes, but take your time. If he's not here, I'll find something to do. Don't worry about me; stay as long as you want."

She reached over and touched his hand. "Thanks for understanding. I hope you don't feel too bad about missing the party."

Leela leaned over and kissed her husband's cheek. She hopped out of the car and stood for a second to watch him make his way down to the end of the driveway. Once he had turned toward the back of the property, she began the short trek up to the front door.

The view of the lake from the front of the house was nice, but the memory of parties on the covered patio, and the view of the glistening water as the sun was going down in the backyard was even better. They'd had some good times with the Thomas family. She wondered what their new status would mean for the friendship they'd formed over the years.

Leela walked up to the oversized double doors and pressed the doorbell.

Riley was encouraged when he pulled around to the back and saw Bill's Hummer parked near the entrance of the guest house. There was a good chance his buddy was in there and could use some company.

Pulling up behind the massive truck, he parked Leela's car and jumped out. He had tried to call Bill again and got voicemail.

Once he walked up to the door, he heard the TV blaring, so he figured Bill was there.

Riley knocked on the door and waited.

"Who's there?"

"Yo, Bill! Dawg, it's me, Ry. Open the door, Man."

Minutes passed before Riley heard movement on the other side of the door. Not long after, the door swung open and Bill peered out with a hand over his eyes.

"Aey, Dawg; what's up?" Bill said.

The scent of stale liquor hit Riley like a massive wrecking ball. He caught his breath and stepped into the house. Riley followed behind Bill who wore a pair of boxer briefs and a dingy, wife-beater undershirt.

Bill flopped down onto the sofa and used the palm of his hand to dry rub his face.

"Can you believe this bull, Man?" he asked.

"Dawg, what happened? I mean, she put that crap out there, but Leela said she's talking about divorce," Riley said.

"Damn right we're getting divorced. I'm bound to lose a lot, but that's better than living in hell every damn day."

"Bill. What you saying, Man? You know it's cheaper to keep her; y'all need to work that out."

Bill shook his head. "It was about time. Kelly and me, Man, we couldn't stay underground like that. It's gonna get ugly, but I know in the end, this is the right thing."

Riley sat on the edge of the coffee table. With his legs spread wide, he propped his elbows atop his knees and took his head into his hands.

"You know what you're saying, Man?" he asked Bill.

"I'm straight. Me and Kelly talked about what would happen if Sam ever found out. I'll admit it, I wasn't ready for it to go down like it did, but we're gonna bounce back."

"So you referring to you and Kelly as *we* now? Dawg, I didn't know it was that deep," Riley said. He shook his head and looked at his friend with sorrowful eyes.

Bill turned and looked at him. Riley couldn't remember a time he'd seen his friend so serious about anything.

"Man. I'm glad she found out. I hate marriage, and so does Kelly."

"Whoa! Hold up a sec." Riley raised his hand. "Hold up, Bruh. Ain't she married, too?"

Bill's face broke into a sly grin. "That was the beauty of it, Man. When both people have a lot to lose, things don't get out of hand.

Well, unless one somebody's wife starts investigating and puts both on blast. Now, not only is my job in jeopardy, but chances are, Kelly's shit is jacked up, too."

"Dawg, I told you, Man, you need to handle your business better. You gotta let these chicks know who's in charge." It was all too much for Riley to digest.

"So you and Bill are just throwing in the towel?" Leela asked.

She knew the answer to her question, but there was something so incredibly unbelievable about the entire situation, both, with Big Mama, and her best friend, Samantha.

Leela had been holed up inside the master suite with Samantha for more than an hour.

"Why does it have to be over? Divorce is so final," Leela said.

Samantha shrugged. "It's time. Honestly, I'm tired. I'm tired of lying next to someone whom I know is screwing anything with a hole. I get it. I really, really get it. There's a shortage of good black men. You give that man a seven-figure, or hell, even six-figure salary, and these women don't know how to act. I'm tired of the rat race. They can have my man because it's exhausting trying to stay two steps ahead of these thirsty heifers."

"You don't want to fight for your marriage?" Leela asked. The wonderment in her voice was difficult to mask. She was bewildered by Samantha's nonchalant approach to ending her ten-year marriage. Sure, there were things about Riley that Leela didn't like. His macho approach to everything worked her last nerve at times. And the fact that everything had to be his way or no way at all wasn't ideal, but nobody was perfect. Leela felt like one mistake shouldn't end a marriage.

Sucking her teeth and rolling her eyes, Samantha looked at Leela side-eyed, and asked, "Aren't you tired?"

"Tired of what?" Leela asked.

She thought she'd come over and offer a comforting ear to Samantha, maybe convince her to go to counseling with Bill. But after nearly two hours with Samantha, Leela knew her efforts would be useless.

Samantha's mind was completely made up.

"Leela, do you really think your husband is faithful? Bill, Riley, think about their circle; they all run together. You know good and well, if thirsty females are throwing it at Bill, they're definitely throwing it at Riley too. Girl, I'm just tired. I can't take it anymore, so he can go be with Kelly, Susan, Keisha, and anybody else he wants. As long as I get my half, I don't give a damn what he does."

Leela said very little.

"The only reason I stayed in as long as I did is because of the way I knew people would react."

Leela's eyebrows elevated.

"Don't tell me you've never shamed anyone who wanted to end a relationship," Samantha quipped. "When you're married, people expect you to do everything to fight for your marriage. My question is, how do you guys know I haven't fought? Maybe I'm tired and ready to take off the gloves. Why should I stay with my husband even if I'm not happy? I've been unhappy for several years and even though we shared more happy years than bad years, why not cut our losses and move on. Everyone deserves to be happy. I'm not a bad person, or a loser, just because I want out of this marriage."

Leela listened as Samantha went on about how married life was no longer for her, and how she'd finally seen the light.

But as she listened, she also thought about the fact that Samantha seemed determined to end the marriage. While Leela didn't agree with Samantha, she told herself it was time to respect her friend's position.

CHAPTER 5

The evening with the Thomases was like nothing Leela or Riley had ever experienced. By the time they left, both were equally depressed. Tension in the car was thick and heavy. The ride back to their house was unusually quiet.

"It's probably best that those two go their separate ways," Riley finally blurted out.

He spoke cautiously, but his words sounded like he had clearly staked his alliance.

"You can say that again. Samantha's got this warped idea that because there's such a shortage of men, expecting you guys to be faithful is like believing in Santa Claus and the tooth fairy."

Leela told herself to ignore the slight flinch she thought she saw at the corner of her husband's right eye. There was no reason she should let Samantha's insecurities become her problem. Their marriages had always been different, and there was no reason to start looking for similarities now.

"She's bitter," Riley finally said. He kept his focus straight ahead as he drove. "I hate that Bill fell for someone else, 'cause that's gonna make things worse for her, but he feels like she's about to take him to the cleaners."

"You're not blaming her, are you?" Leela asked.

Riley shrugged. At first, he didn't respond to his wife's comment.

"I mean, she has every right to be bitter," Leela added.

"Does she really?" Riley looked at her. "Let's look at the facts. She invaded his privacy, had him followed, shamed him in front of everyone we know, then embarrassed him further by putting everything she found on social media sites for everyone in America to see. Now, my man could lose his job, all because of some shit she pulled."

"What's his job got to do with this?" Leela asked. She was confused by the connection, but more concerned that Riley didn't point at the affair which led to Samantha's so-called bitterness.

"You know what we do. We work for a private brokerage firm. There's a morality clause in the contract, and now he's been put on leave. A bunch of his clients started calling and complaining almost immediately."

"Wow!" Leela said.

Samantha mentioned the status of Bill's job over the phone, but in person, her main focus was on plans to sell their house and the amount of assets she would get.

"I'm sure she didn't think that move through all the way," Leela added.

"Ya' think! Then on top of that, Bill says she refuses to take that crap down. So not only are his dirty deeds out there for everyone to see, but she won't take it down. I told him from jump, he didn't need to have her doing his social media campaign," Riley said.

"I think she should take it down too, but I could see why he trusted her to handle that. It's what she does. But still, despite the details of how it all went down, I don't think we should be taking sides," said Leela.

"If you ask me, there are no sides here; it's obvious she was wrong for dragging my man's name through the mud like that. But it's gonna backfire on her anyway. He's gonna lose a lot behind her little stunt, and if he loses, so does she."

"You act like he wasn't wrong for screwing around on his wife!" Leela snarled. "Let's not forget. He screwed another woman, lied about it continuously, and tried to make his wife think she was crazy for even suggesting that there might be something going on with him and Kelly," Leela said. "You do see where he was at fault, right?"

She noticed her husband flinch, and silently, she dared him to defend his friend's actions as it related to the affair.

CHAPTER 6

"Yeah, Dawg. What's up?"

Riley knew the call was from Bill because his number popped up on the cell phone screen. But there was no sound on the other end of the phone.

"Bill? What's up?" Riley called out again. He was on his way to the parking garage after work, when his cell phone rang, but he waited to get on the elevator for fear the call would drop.

As he was about to hang up, he heard a faint voice.

"Bill? That you, Dawg?"

"Yeah. Uh, can you come scoop me? I'm downtown 'bout to leave the DoubleTree. You know where it is?"

Bill's voice had dropped a few octaves, but the more he talked, the clearer he became. Riley had lots of questions, but felt they could wait since he'd see him soon.

"Yeah. You just caught me. I'll be there in ten; lemme grab my ride," Riley said.

"Bet that."

Behind the wheel of his Cadillac Escalade, Riley tried to coach himself on how to handle his friend's constant ups and downs. He wanted to be supportive, but Bill made it challenging at times. He needed him to man-up!

Bill was waiting curbside, so it was easy for Riley to slow down and allow him to hop into the passenger's side of the truck.

Bill looked disheveled, needed a trim, and his clothes were wrinkled.

For a man who prided himself on his meticulous appearance at all times, Riley could hardly believe the change in his friend. Riley made a mental note to talk to him about it at a later time.

"What's up, Man?" Riley asked.

He maneuvered the truck into traffic and waited for the predictable sob-story from Bill. He'd become accustomed to it ever since the divorce proceedings had started.

"Bruh, this crap with Kelly is about to kill me. She ain't leaving, Man."

Riley's eyebrows rose. He clutched the steering wheel tighter and focused on the road.

"Can you believe that shit? For more than a year, we've been hot and heavy. Now that I'm single, she's talking about maybe we should chill!"

"Don't you think it kinda makes sense?" Riley asked. "I mean, the investigation is still underway, right?"

"Dude. She's talking about staying with her husband! After my shit was blown all out the water, I thought we had an understanding. I thought, given the opportunity, we'd be together," Bill said.

Riley turned to look at him. "Man. You sounding real suspect right now. You weren't trying to jump right into something else before the divorce is final, were you?" Riley shook his head. "That's probably not a good move."

"What difference does it make? As soon as Sam agrees to the terms, we'll be divorced. She's getting what she wants, so she's not tripping. When Kelly told me to meet her at the hotel, I didn't think it was so she could dump me!" Bill sighed.

"So it's over between you two then?" Riley asked. "Kelly, I mean?"

"Yeah. Seems I'm not all that irresistible after all, since I'm single now. Go figure."

The entire situation was a mess. Riley couldn't believe how

emotional Bill was being. So Kelly didn't want him; he could simply find another chick that did. Riley didn't see the problem, but the way his boy was looking, Riley kept his thoughts to himself.

"She should've said she wouldn't leave dude no matter what," Bill muttered.

Riley's eyebrows went up, but he didn't say anything else about it. He silently wished Bill would do the same.

For Leela, alone time became time to reflect. She had a lot to reflect on. All she could think about was that last lunch with her mother and grandmother.

Lunch with her mother and grandmother was usually a good time over colorful cocktails and an array of scrumptious appetizers. In the past, Big Mama was the center of attention. But everything was different at their last lunch meeting. And different was not good in this instance. Leela couldn't shake the memory that took her right back to that restaurant.

Gloom hung over their table like a dark cloud on a bright summer day. From the moment Beverly rose to hug her, Leela noticed her grandmother's features were clouded with concern.

There was no sign of her usual vibrant smile, and her weary face wore a sad expression. It was as if her grandmother had aged more than a decade since the last time she'd seen her, two weeks prior. Leela felt so bad for her.

"I'm gonna need a drink before you start, Big Mama," Linda said. She looked at her daughter and said, "You should get one too."

Leela looked at her mother and dismissed the suggestion. She wanted a clear head so she could decipher what was about to be said. It was usually Linda who broke any family-related news—good, bad, or devastating.

But this time, all Linda did was carry on about how life was about to change.

Leela had been haunted by the revelation for days, that something major was about to happen. She only backed off from talking about it because her mother had all but begged her not to ask any questions or say anything. Linda explained it would hurt her grandmother and that was all it took for Leela to leave it alone.

"Leela. You remember Miss Sadie down the street, right?" her grandmother Beverly began.

"Of course. You two have been friends for years; we practically grew up with her daughter, and Rhonda's kids," Leela said. "Rhonda. She's like your age, right, Mom? You guys went to school together?"

Linda's lips were pursed together before she brought the glass up to her mouth. She rolled her eyes and turned her attention back to Big Mama.

"Well, apparently your grandfather is the father of Rhonda's kids," Beverly said.

Leela heard what was said, but she needed the words not to be true. They didn't make sense.

"What?"

Leela looked back and forth between her mother and grandmother; confusion was all over her face. Suddenly, she regretted not getting that drink.

"Rhonda? How…" Leela's voice trailed off. Suddenly, a thumping headache came out of nowhere. Leela felt lost.

"Now you know how I felt," said Linda. "All the times she and her illiterate, illegitimate kids came around like we were all just good neighbors and the trick was secretly screwing my daddy!" Linda smirked. "You better than me, Big Mama, 'cause I woulda cut 'em all!"

"Wait. When was all of this going on? Big Mama, didn't Rhonda used to bring her kids over to the house? You babysat them, and all along she knew your husband was their father?" Leela asked. Words scraped the back of Leela's throat as she struggled to grasp the situation. She swallowed back tears.

"Honey, that's what we've discovered," Beverly said.

Leela watched her grandmother closely. Her poise and elegant manner remained fully intact. When she told the story of the ultimate betrayal and heartbreak, she did so with a peaceful and relaxed tone. She'd always been the calm and laid-back type, but the story she told was enough to drive anyone over the edge. In that moment, Leela admired her grandmother even more.

"I wanted to whup that bitch's ass!" Linda said. "Then her half-senile mama over there crying every day, asking how did she go wrong. It's like they're all crazy!" Linda chimed in between sips.

"Wait. Rhonda had a drug problem. Why would he?" Leela asked. The question was rhetorical, and she barely realized she had verbalized it.

"Yes. She did. She ran off for a few years, but that stuff really had a hold on her," Beverly said. "I never would've thought my husband was doing anything but helping over there. You know Sadie never married and she seemed okay about it. I didn't even mind your grandfather helping out. I figured that was doing the right thing. Everyone needs a man around the house."

"Big Mama. Rhonda's kids spent so much time with us!" Leela added. She was stunned. She couldn't make sense of it no matter how hard she tried.

"Yeah. I remember that. I remember you and the church really banding around Miss Sadie," said Linda.

"After fifty-two years of marriage," Leela muttered. She shook her head slowly. "For all thirty-four of my years, I've never known another marriage like yours."

"It's unbelievable to us all, Honey." Beverly took Leela's hand.

But Linda remained defiant. "That goes to show you," Linda said. "When all is said and done, ain't none of 'em loyal!"

SNAP!

SNAP!

"What the hell, Leela?!"

Riley snapped his fingers as if to pull Leela back to the present.

"Oh. Babe. I'm sorry." Leela shook her head.

"You didn't hear me talking to you?"

"What did you say?"

Riley gave his wife a stern look.

"I know. The whole answer the question with a question thing," Leela said.

"So how long do I have to come in and find my wife staring off into space? You act like it's the end of the world. I need you to get over it, dammit!"

Leela couldn't remember how long she'd been zoned out. If she didn't dream about that lunch with Big Mama and Linda, she thought about the video of Bill and his mistress. She felt like her mind was slowly slipping away.

It didn't help that Samantha carried on as if nothing in her life had changed, but now that her own husband's frustrations were growing, Leela knew she needed to do something and she needed to take action quickly.

CHAPTER 7

When Leela learned her best friend's divorce was final, she still couldn't wrap her mind around it. And while she'd heard and seen horror stories about life after divorce, Samantha's battle scars were very hard to find.

The bright-colored wrap dress that hugged Samantha's shapely, statuesque, size-13 figure made her stand out as she maneuvered her way through a throng of people near the bar. Samantha had always turned heads, so that was nothing new to Leela, but for a person who just officially ended a ten-year marriage, the girl looked bad!

"Hey, Boo!" Samantha approached the table, and breezed in like she didn't have a single care.

"Wow! You look fab!" Leela said.

"Don't sound so surprised. Get up and give me some love; act like you ain't seen me in nearly two whole weeks!" Samantha said.

Leela rose and fell into her friend's embrace. They were meeting for dinner at Pappadeaux off I-10. As they settled into their seats and took in the hustle and bustling sounds of the busy restaurant, Leela couldn't help but compare the two divorcees in her life.

For one, it looked like the move had ushered new life into her. Samantha had always been attractive, but she didn't believe in going the extra mile when it came to her appearance. Now, however, she looked different, and in a very good way. She was stunning in her outfit and new makeup.

But for her grandmother, who had for the very first time in her life, moved into her own one-bedroom apartment, divorce looked completely different. Big Mama rarely ventured out, and that forced Linda to set up a schedule to pull her out to lunch or out for shopping.

Big Mama was no longer connected to her church, and unless Linda or Leela insisted, she tried to remain holed up inside the apartment. The apartment stayed dark with the blinds and drapes closed night and day.

"Maybe she should go talk to somebody," Leela suggested the last time she and her mother talked about Big Mama.

"Girl, ain't nothing wrong with her but a broken heart. You know how many times I've been divorced?" Linda asked.

Leela knew it was a rhetorical question, but still. Her mother's lighthearted approach to everything sometimes rubbed her the wrong way.

"Ma. You might hold the Guinness World Record for the number of divorces for any one woman, but you've gotta remember, Big Mama was married to the same man for fifty-two years!"

That shut her mother up—temporarily.

"I may have to downsize my lifestyle, but that's okay. Thank God we didn't have any kids," Samantha said with a small whistle and a wide-eyed grin.

Her comment brought Leela's attention back to their table. Leela couldn't get over how quickly and seamlessly her friend seemed to be moving on.

Their first appetizer arrived and they dug in. Leela had ordered as she waited on Samantha to arrive.

Once the waiter walked away, Samantha leaned in. "I had a date the other night and I have to admit, it felt kind of strange."

"Oh, I can imagine. You were married for a long time," Leela said. "I'll bet it was odd to be out with another man, after being with Bill for so long. Did it make you realize you do miss him a little?" Leela bit into a Shrimp Brochette.

The bewilderment on Samantha's face gave Leela pause.

"Oh…I'm sorry, I didn't mean to go on talking about what must've been a real emotional event for you," Leela quickly added.

Samantha drew her eyebrows together. "Umm. It was nothing like that. I was just wondering whether it was socially acceptable these days to go down on a man on the first date."

Samantha's comment was met with a blank stare. Leela was speechless. She wasn't sure how to even respond.

After a long and awkward stretch of silence, Samantha shrugged and bit into a shrimp. The waiter had returned at the perfect time.

"Oh. You and Riley doing okay?" Samantha asked after the waiter left the table with their drink orders.

"Of course; why do you ask?" Leela didn't know Samantha was already dating, and obviously having sex. She welcomed the subject change because she didn't want to sound like the prude she felt like.

"Oh. No reason. I'm just glad that after all you've been through between Big Mama and me, that you guys are still doing good." Samantha's eyes followed Leela's. "What's the matter?"

Leela frowned. "I could've sworn I just saw Natasha." Samantha whipped her head in both directions. Her eyes searched the room, but she didn't see anyone who looked like Natasha.

"Natasha, as in…"

"Yes. That Natasha," Leela said. "Natasha stalker-bitch Robinson! You know what, I can't be sure of anything anymore. It probably wasn't even her." Leela took a sip. "Now, what were you saying?"

Natasha was Riley's ex. It didn't end well, and Leela only got peace after the woman picked up and moved because she couldn't get over the fact that Riley had moved on.

Samantha scanned the room again before she spoke. She was looking for Natasha too, but suddenly, her eyes connected with a handsome man who didn't flinch or attempt to look away when her gaze stopped on him. As a matter-of-fact, his stare overpowered hers, until she finally looked away.

"I was just saying that with all that's going on, me and Bill and Big Mama, I wanted to make sure you and Riley are doing okay."

Leela found the comment kind of strange, but she didn't want to talk about her marriage. She wanted to know what life was like for Samantha now that she was living life as a single woman.

"Soooo, people go all the way on a first date now?" Leela asked sheepishly.

Samantha cracked up with laughter.

"Girl, I'm sure I've broken every dating rule in the book over the last few weeks. The guy was fine as all get-out. He was packing, and I wanted some." Samantha shrugged. "So, I got some. Oh. I almost forgot to tell you! Next March, I'm going on the Tom Joyner Cruise," Samantha squealed.

With her eyebrow raised, Leela put down the warm bread she was about to bite into. "What?"

"Yup! You heard me. I screwed the guy; I hardly remember his name. I felt so free, so liberated, I was like, why stop there with a one-night stand. I guess it was the thrill of doing something so taboo for me, so I figured, why not do something completely uncharacteristic. I know, we've joked about it for years, but I finally said, what the hell, why not go on the cruise? I no longer have to answer to a warden anymore, so what the hell?" Samantha shrugged. "Who knows, I may even have another one-night stand while I'm on the ship!"

"I can't believe it." Leela's voice was kind of somber.

Wrinkling her nose, Samantha said, "Girrl, me either! Who

knew a one-night stand would be so thrilling! Can you believe I'm nearly forty and I had never had a one-night stand?"

"I'm not talking about that! I'm talking about the cruise!"

"Oh. That. Yeah, I'm real hyped about that too."

The revelation left Leela feeling peculiar. She couldn't figure out why, but a small part of her felt envy when she thought about her best friend's new single status and all the fun and exciting things she was now able to do. She didn't envy the casual sex, but the thought of going on vacation alone or even with Samantha was quite enticing. It was also something she knew for sure her husband would never agree to.

Soon, two drinks were delivered to their table. Samantha didn't have to look up at the handsome stranger to know they were compliments of him and his equally gorgeous friend.

When Riley's cell phone rang, he didn't want to look at it, much less answer. He was tired of Bill and his woe-is-me attitude.

Each Friday, he tried to leave work a little early to have a few brews with his boy before he called it a night and went home. Most of those outings ended fine with Riley making it in well before midnight, but after last Friday, he started to wonder whether they should find something else to do.

"It's about time," he said when the phone stopped ringing. But a few minutes later, the phone rang again.

"Aey, Dawg. Let's go to this new spot in Third Ward," Bill said the second Riley answered.

"I don't know. I was thinking about sitting it out tonight, Playboy," Riley said.

"Nah, Dawg! Nah. I'm telling you. You'll like this spot."

Riley was reluctant, but Bill sounded so desperate. Riley knew he was probably lonely considering he was divorced and his girlfriend had dumped him.

"C'mon, Man. This place is real chill, I'm telling you. The honeys be in the house, and they even got a live band tonight," he said.

Riley found it hard to ignore the desperation in his boy's voice. He didn't like it, but he knew it was real. Long before the divorce was final, it seemed like Bill was focused on being out and seen as much as possible, and he wanted Riley at his side.

"All right, look. I'll roll, but I'm not trying to stay out too late," Riley said.

Hours later, Riley was a little pissed when he pulled up at 3000 Blodgett Street in Houston's Third Ward. It was where he and Bill had agreed to meet.

The area, in Houston's historic part of town, was hit and miss, with a combination of lounges and dive bars. Some places were nice, and others were far less so.

Inside, the brisk air-conditioned breeze was a welcomed relief.

Riley walked up to the bar and ordered a beer. He looked around the small interior and took in the sleek ambiance. A DJ was perched near the front door behind a long table that held several large aluminum containers. A small line of people gathered near it, for the complimentary catfish and fries.

"Hey, Dawg, how long you been here?"

Picking up the green bottle, Riley extended it toward Bill and said, "I was about to leave after this if you hadn't showed up. This is my second."

"Aw, Man. Well, I'm here now. Sorry about the wait; I was at my lawyer's office when we talked earlier."

Bill was still in a battle trying to save his job. He had hired an attorney, and it looked like he might be successful, but it was taking time.

"The next round is on me," he said to Riley.

"Cool. Bet that," Riley said.

At first Riley felt bad that he was reluctant to hang out with his boy. They talked about the upcoming game Sunday night and ate some of the fish and fries. He finally felt like he needed to relax and enjoy his time out with his boy.

"Can we get another round?" Bill asked the female bartender.

Once their drinks were refreshed, Riley turned to look out at the growing crowd. Bill didn't exaggerate when he said the honeys would be out in force. The women outnumbered the men by at least five to one, and any real man could appreciate those odds.

Riley was settling in for a nice evening when the door opened and in walked Kelly. Riley looked over at Bill, then at his friend's former mistress, and suddenly it hit him that he'd been set up.

CHAPTER 8

Later that night, Leela applied moisturizer to her arms and legs after a hot shower. She sat on her side of the bed while her husband went down to make sure the house was secure. It was nearly one in the morning, and he had only been home for about thirty minutes.

"Dinner with Samantha was interesting this evening," she said, once Riley walked into their room and closed the door.

"Oh, yeah? How so?" he asked.

From his tone, Leela could tell he wasn't really that interested in a conversation about her best friend, but she wanted to make conversation.

"She looked really good. I mean, like I've never seen her look so put together," Leela said.

Her husband's broad shoulders hunched. "Well, she is back on the market now," he said. "Guess it makes sense."

"Yeah. I guess so. She seems so different now."

"Babe." Riley turned to face his wife. "They're both two different people now. To be honest with you, I don't know what's going on with Bill. He had me meet him at a place where I think he knew Kelly was gonna be."

"What?"

"Yeah. The shit was kind of foul. She shows up to meet some dude and the dude was not her husband. It seems like when she told Bill she was gonna stay with her husband, she only meant that she didn't want to be with him. It was bad. We barely got out of there without a major scene jumping off," Riley said.

"Wait. So he thought Kelly was gonna leave her husband because he and Samantha got a divorce?"

"I guess so. But from what I saw tonight, ol' girl ain't thinking about Bill. She was there with her new man all out in public like she was single."

"How'd you get Bill to leave?"

"I told him I wasn't about to get caught up in any kind of drama. He didn't want to leave, but I told him, we needed to bounce and I was leaving without him if he wanted to stay."

"So if you guys left, why'd you get home so late?"

"The only way he'd agree to leave was if I promised to swing by Sugar Hill for a drink with him," Riley said.

"Oh. I see. Well, you know how I feel about you doing all that drinking, then getting behind the wheel and driving all the way out here to Katy," Leela said.

"I was good. You know I'm not getting behind the wheel if I think I've had too much," Riley said.

"But that's the thing, Ry. You won't know when you've had too much. All I know is, you've been going out a lot more now that Bill is single again. I don't want his new status to become a DWI charge for you; that's all I'm saying, Babe."

Riley whipped around and roared at his wife. "Do I say anything when you run off and go hang out with Samantha's bitter ass?"

"Whoa, Ry!" Leela threw her hands up in mock defense.

"Whoa, my ass! Don't come for me. It's not necessary. I just told you dude needed some time. You somehow turn this into something about me. I don't need you to warn me about the dangers of drinking and driving." Riley slapped his chest. "I'm a man!"

"What am I missing here?" Leela asked.

"You know what, I don't need this shit." Riley snatched a pillow and stormed out of their bedroom.

Leela sat dumbfounded and alone. The last thing she wanted was alone time. Being alone had quickly become her enemy. It didn't take long for thoughts of her grandfather's betrayal to seep into her mind. It was so long ago, Leela couldn't remember how old she and her sister were, but they were arriving at their grandparents' house when their neighbor, Rhonda's mother, had called with an emergency.

"Big Mama, what are Miss Sadie's grandkids doing over here? I told you I needed you to watch Leela and Leslie," Linda had said as she dropped Leela and her older sister off.

"I know, but Sadie just called and asked if I could keep 'em overnight. Your father went out to try and help find Rhonda."

"Not again." Linda had sucked her teeth and put the overnight bag down on the sofa. "Them poor kids. It don't matter how many times Daddy tracks her down and drags her back to Miss Sadie's. That crack is way more powerful than Daddy and Miss Sadie put together."

"Linda, hush now! Not in front of the kids. They can't help that their Mama is sick."

"She ain't sick; she's a crackhead, Big Mama."

"Linda! I said hush your mouth!"

"Okay, Big Mama, okay. You ain't gotta go getting all worked up. But the truth is the truth. We ain't gotta talk about it, and just because we don't, that don't mean Rhonda ain't a crackhead."

"Shoo." Big Mama had waved her arm toward the door. "Don't you have somewhere you need to be? Get on up out of here before you upset these kids."

"Big Mama, we old enough to be home by ourselves. I don't

know why Mama don't trust us. Leslie is almost sixteen," Leela had said.

Rhonda's son, Darnell, had run into the kitchen. The nipple of his bottle hung between his teeth and he squealed with laughter.

"Get on out of here, Linda. What time you coming by to pick up the girls?"

Linda had shrugged and shuffled out of the front door.

Leela remembered being around Rhonda's kids throughout her teenage and young adult years. There were times when Rhonda was clean for months on end; then one day, she'd vanish.

Miss Sadie would show up with a sad story and Pah-pah would leave to go help look for her. Leela shook the memory from her thoughts. She adjusted herself on the bed, stabbed at her pillow, and squeezed her eyes shut.

She was determined to get some sleep. No more thoughts of her grandparents, Samantha and Bill, or even Riley.

CHAPTER 9

Leela felt like she was being pulled in several directions and none of them was where she wanted to be. By the time she got up and moving Saturday morning, Riley was gone.

She knew he probably left to go play basketball with his friends like he did most Saturday mornings, but the fact that he left without looking in on her was hurtful.

Her phone rang. Before she reached for it, she knew it would either be her mother or Samantha. After Samantha's revelation that she'd be going on a cruise they'd both daydreamed of doing for years, Leela wondered whether their friendship would survive Samantha's new single status.

"Hey, Ma, I'm getting ready to walk out the door now," she said into the phone, once she realized it was her mother calling.

"Okay. I was just calling to let you know we've changed restaurants," Linda said.

Once she got the updated location, Leela left the house and thought again about her husband. Sadly, she admitted to herself that something wasn't right with Riley. Leela didn't know whether she was feeling emotional because of how he left the house or if she was internalizing everyone else's issues.

She arrived at the restaurant and rushed to greet Big Mama and her mother. Leela placed her purse onto the back of the chair and settled into her seat. "How's Pah-pah?"

The moment the question left her lips, Leela felt like she had somehow betrayed her grandmother.

"You know you can call him and find out," Big Mama said.

Leela looked at her grandmother, but her eyes quickly darted to her mother when she spoke.

"I wouldn't call that filthy dog," Linda said about her father.

Big Mama looked between the two and focused her attention on her granddaughter. "This is gonna be a challenge for all of us and it's not gonna be easy, but it's perfectly okay for you to continue your relationship with your grandfather."

Linda's face contorted into a frown. "Oh no the hell it's not," she howled.

"Linda. Yes it is. You're gonna have to find a way to forgive your father. He's the only father you have, and it's not fair for you to push your feelings off on your daughter."

"Big Mama. After all he did to you, to this family? I don't think any of us should be talking to him ever again."

"Well, you're not being realistic. You know your father's health is failing, and he's gonna need support from his kids," Big Mama said.

Linda sucked her teeth. She didn't give her mother much pushback, but Leela knew for sure that her mother meant it when she said she wanted nothing else to do with her father.

"How have you been? How was it this week?" Leela asked her grandmother.

"It's hard. You know I left my parents' house for my husband's. I still think about him each and every day. I was prepared for until-death-do-us-part. He's the only man I've ever loved," Big Mama said.

Her words broke Leela's heart. She reached for her grandmother's hand and squeezed tightly.

"I keep telling her she needs to get out more. But maybe you just need yourself a little young buck," Linda joked.

Leela and Big Mama looked at her, but failed to see the humor in her joke.

"Wwwwaaahht?" Linda squealed. "Lots of older women are hooking up with younger men. It's the in thing now." Linda shrugged off the awkward glances. "Twist up your faces if you want to, but I'll take a younger man over one my age any day or night of the week."

Big Mama's sudden outburst of laughter caught everyone off guard. "Chile, I'm seventy-two years old. I don't care what these other women are doing. What would I do with some younger man?"

"Don't knock it 'til you try it, Big Mama," Linda joked, then winked.

Leela didn't say another word. But her mind raced with thoughts of what would become of her grandmother who after fifty-two years of marriage was now divorced and left to fend for herself.

After brunch with her mother and grandmother, Leela left to meet Samantha at a new hair shop they'd been dying to try. Thereafter, the plan was to grab a quick drink and appetizers before Leela headed back home.

"You can go home, but I'm going to see Monique; then I'm going to the after-party," Samantha announced when they discussed their plans.

Leela wasn't about to entertain the idea. She knew most of Riley's day would be consumed by basketball games, but once he got home, cleaned up, and rested, he'd be ready for them to do something together.

This new single-lady lifestyle was definitely gonna take some getting used to for Leela.

Riley hated being in a pissing contest with Bill, but since the divorce, it seemed that was what most of their conversations had turned into. The current one was about to drive him crazy.

"Dawg, you lying," Bill taunted Riley.

"What I gotta lie to you for?" Riley asked as he took another healthy swig from his beer.

"So you tryin' to make me believe that you really believe your wife has been completely faithful to you in the whole time y'all been together?" The wonder in Bill's voice was apparent.

Riley shrugged. "I ain't tryin' to make you believe anything. I'm just telling you that I ain't never had a woman cheat on me."

When Kelly decided to drop Bill, Riley felt like it sent his boy into a downward spiral of self-doubt. Somehow, that made his friend question just about everything about the opposite sex.

"Bullshit!" Bill yelled. "Bullshit. All women cheat, Dawg," he insisted.

"Nah, they don't, just like all men don't cheat," Riley said smugly.

Bill tossed Riley a wicked glare as a smirk spread across his face. "Oh, so what about my bachelor party?" he asked.

"What about it?" Riley challenged.

"I remember that stripper, the little chocolate-colored one with the phat ass and massive tits. She was all on your tip. You can't tell me you didn't hit that," Bill said.

"I wasn't married at the time," Riley said. "But what's that got to do with anything? Man, I don't feel like talking about this shit all the time. I'm about to get you some Midol; lately, all you wanna do is sit around and talk about your damn feelings, and emotions and shit."

"Why you going there, Dawg?"

"That's you, Man. Hell, ever since you saw Kelly with that other dude, you just wanna sit up talking about cheating and all that crap.

Man up! She ain't the only chick out there; go get some new ass and get over it!"

"It ain't even like that," Bill defended.

"Really? 'Cause I can't tell."

"I'm good, Dawg."

"Really, you good? Then why we always talking about feelings and shit like that? We don't even talk about the game anymore. Look, don't worry about what's going on in my house; I got that handled. You should know that by now."

"I feel you; I feel you; but ain't it boring?" Bill asked.

Riley took a sip from his bottle and thought before he answered. "Ain't what boring?"

"You sleeping with the same woman over and over again, year in, year out."

"I mean, it ain't like fireworks jumping off or anything like it was in the beginning. And most times, she acts like it's a chore to give me some, but it's all good," Riley admitted.

Bill's head shook like it was set on automatic. He listened with a look of pity across his face. "Damn, Man. You don't have to explain to me. I was married for ten damn years! I know what it's like. They fall into a rut and soon, you've gotta beg them for what's rightfully yours."

"Look, Dude, why we talking about this? You messing up my high," Riley admonished.

"We ain't gotta talk about it anymore, but just know I have a new mission and it's one I take very seriously," Bill said.

"Whatchu' talkin' 'bout, Willis?" Riley asked, mocking a scene from one of their favorite old-time TV sitcoms, *Diff'rent Strokes.*

"I'm on a mission to get you some ass on the side!" Bill said.

"Oh hell naw. You see where that got you, right? I'm good. If I want something different, I'll just use the old reliable," Riley said.

Bill frowned. "The old reliable?"

Riley raised his palm and they both laughed at his implication.

"But on the real though, we can put this to rest once and for all, if you game," Bill said.

Riley twisted his lips. He mulled over what Bill was talking about for a second. He leaned in and said, "So lemme get this straight. I hear you out and we can finally put an end to all these emotional discussions you always wanna have?"

"Yeah, something like that," Bill said. "I mean, that's only if you man enough; since you got so much faith in your woman and all."

Riley shrugged. "Shit, if I'm man enough? Well, we don't need to go any further because everybody knows, I'm the man, and I'm game."

"Okay. Bet that."

CHAPTER 10

Leela felt like a fool as she walked around her massive, elegant home. With her hair freshly done, and experiencing a slight buzz, she regretted opting to go home versus out on the town with Samantha. The house was completely empty and she was alone.

She had rushed through drinks and appetizers with Samantha because she didn't want her husband to return to an empty home and he hadn't even made an appearance.

What was most frustrating was the fact that he never even called to let her know he'd be out through the night. The few times that she called him, voicemail kicked in immediately.

She was hesitant to call her mother or even Samantha. She knew that a call to Samantha would turn into one big *I told you so.*

Earlier, it was all she could do to get out of the restaurant and not be dragged into Samantha's Saturday night plans, although it was tempting.

She walked into the kitchen in hopes of being inspired to fix something to eat, but the phone rang before she could get started. It was Linda. Leela sighed, but she took the call.

"Hey, you talk to Big Mama this evening?"

Leela's heart sank. "No, why? What's wrong? Did something happen?" This wasn't the kind of excitement she needed on a Saturday night.

"Nothing, just wondering why she ain't answering the phone, that's all. It's nothing. What you and Riley doing tonight?"

Leela pulled the phone from her ear and looked at it. Was her mother bored or something?

"Ah, actually, he's not here. So I'm gonna meet up with Samantha later."

"Oh… you know I never did get all the goods on what went down with those two. So he really cheated on her, huh?"

It was the way Linda asked that gave Leela pause. They were all there together, and it was Linda who helped clear the house, so she knew for sure that Linda saw the same video.

"Yeah, you know he did. You were at the party."

"Umph. Well, all I've gotta say is, if that video was accurate, she may have wanted to hang on to that one," Linda remarked.

Leela wanted the conversation to end, but she wasn't that fortunate.

"From what I could see, they don't make 'em like him anymore," Linda said.

Leela was disgusted. She was more than relieved when Linda put her on hold to take another call. The instant Linda clicked over, Leela ended the call and decided she wouldn't answer when her mother called back.

As she thought back to her time with Samantha, regret began to seep in. Why didn't she throw caution to the wind and go out with her? She should've done the unexpected.

"What's stopping me from doing it now?" she asked aloud.

Leela grabbed her cell and dialed Samantha.

"Hey, girl, is everything okay?!" Samantha yelled. She finally answered on the third phone call. The music in the background was so loud and so overpowering, Leela struggled to hear her.

"Everything is fine. I've changed my mind; where are you?" Leela asked.

"Hmm?"

"I said, where are you?"

"Where am I? Why? Are you gonna come out tonight?"

"Yes, where are you?"

"Oh. I'm at Belvedere!" Samantha yelled over the music. It took her repeating it a few times before Leela finally understood.

"Okay. I'll see you soon."

Leela had never been to Belvedere, but she looked forward to going out instead of staying home alone. Leela walked into the closet and pulled out a white, slinky, sleeveless sweater dress that fit like a second layer of skin. She put on a pair of sky-high, nude-colored stilettos and grabbed a multicolored wristlet on her way out.

After she punched the address to Belvedere into her car's navigation system, she took off. To get herself into a party mood, she turned on the latest hip-hop station and started to groove to the music.

Leela pulled up to valet parking and stepped out of her car when the young guy extended a hand to her.

"Welcome to Belvedere," he said. "You look lovely this evening."

"Thank you." Leela accepted the claim ticket he gave her and walked into the sleek lounge. Immediately, she was pulled in by the space and its similarities to Miami. Its neon-lit rooms screamed South Beach and Leela loved it instantly.

She texted Samantha and let her know she was walking in. Three steps in and Samantha appeared.

"You did the damn thing!" Samantha screamed over the loud music. "You look hot."

Samantha rushed Leela over to the section where she sat with several friends. Soon, the drinks were flowing and laughter floated all around.

Nearly two hours after she'd been partying, drinking and enjoying the ambiance, her cell phone vibrated. Leela looked down and saw her husband's number flash across the screen. She ran a perfectly manicured finger across the screen and declined the call. As far as she was concerned, he was too late. It was her turn to let loose.

"Oh no! Put that phone down; it's time to party!" Samantha yelled as she grabbed Leela by the arm and pulled her up.

"Wait. Let me turn it off," Leela said. She powered off her cell phone, stuffed it into her wristlet and followed Samantha to an area where they started to dance.

It wasn't long before two men showed up and started dancing along with them. Leela remembered her handsome partner from a few weeks ago when she and Samantha met for drinks.

Yes, she had made the right move when she decided to join Samantha at Belvedere.

"Ssssh!" Samantha tried to hush her friend as she struggled to keep her upright.

Hours later, the foreign sounds outside his front door alarmed Riley almost instantly. It was 3:45 in the morning and his wife was still not at home. Her cell phone was off because calls had gone directly to voicemail. Riley had been on high alert ever since he pulled into the garage and her car was not there.

He heard laughter and giggles. Then more shushing, followed by more conversation.

When he got up from his spot in the sitting room, he rushed to the door to see what all the commotion was about. He held his pistol behind his back. Cautiously, Riley opened his front door. The first thing that caught his eye was two men waiting in Samantha's car that was parked behind his wife's. Samantha helped Leela out of the car and struggled to walk her to the front door.

"Oh. Hey, Ry. She's had a li'l too much to drink. So my friends helped me get her and her car home," Samantha said.

Riley tucked the gun into the back of his waistband and rushed outside to help Samantha. He gave Samantha the look of death as he took over to help keep his wife on her feet.

"You outta order for this shit," he said, just as Samantha turned to leave. She stopped and looked back at him.

"Excuse me?"

"So now because you ain't got no man, you trying to hook my wife up with other men?" Riley asked. He motioned in the direction of the men who sat in her car.

Samantha followed his gaze to Malone and Kent and a scowl made its way to her face.

"Did you hear me say she was too drunk to drive? My friends were kind enough to offer to help us out," she hissed. "Ah. You're welcome because she could've just crashed on my couch, but she insisted she had to go home."

Riley's eyes narrowed as they took her in. "You know what. I get it now."

"You get what, exactly?" Samantha asked.

"I get your situation. After Bill moved on, you probably felt like the clock was ticking on your pretty face and tiny waist, so you back out there in the rat race again. But look, just because you blew off your marriage, don't try to bring Leela down to where you are," he said.

"Down?" Samantha chuckled. "Does anything about me say I am down and out? You'd better look again because I'm having the time of my life. Actually, life started when I left that loser friend of yours, and I don't sit and watch any clocks. Ain't a damn thing ticking over here! Believe that. And you're welcome for my friends and me bringing your wife home safely."

Without another word, and her head held high, Samantha turned and strutted away.

Left alone, Riley struggled to get Leela up the stairs. She was so drunk her body felt heavier than dead weight. He was pissed, despite the fact that he had arrived home only twenty minutes before Leela. He felt she disrespected their marriage just by being out 'til sunup.

The fact that she had to be brought home by some dudes he didn't know was an even bigger dis. And neither one of them had the decency to get out of the car and say anything to him. That would've been the right thing for a real man to do.

Then look at what she had worn! No way in the world a married woman had any business being out in the streets in some mini-dress showing off all her damn assets.

Once he got her upstairs and into bed, he closed the door and went down to his man-cave to try and calm down. He needed to tell her about the foul behavior and he was gonna take it a step further, too.

Instead of going to sleep, Riley's mind raced with thoughts of how he needed to put his foot down and get his household back in order.

The more he thought about it, the more he convinced himself that he probably didn't need to go in too hard on his wife. If he had to think about some of the things that had happened while he was out with Bill, he knew there would be enough to raise an eyebrow. But, hell, he was a man! That was different. Wives were held to a higher standard, especially his, and Leela knew that.

The next day, it was noon before Leela emerged from the room. Riley was in the kitchen marinating pork chops to grill.

"Hey," he said as his wife walked into the kitchen.

"Ssshhh. My head," Leela complained. She pointed a finger toward her temple.

Riley slammed a pot on the counter top and his wife cringed.

"That's wrong on so many levels," she complained.

"Hey, you should know when to say when," he said loudly.

"Quiet! Use your inside voice, please," Leela begged.

She eased onto one of the high stool chairs and watched as her husband seasoned the meat. He used melted butter to brush over vegetables in a dish, then wrapped baking potatoes in aluminum foil.

When he was finished, he turned to his wife. "This shit has got to stop. If you want to save this marriage, then I think it's time we have a serious and long overdue talk."

CHAPTER 11

The modest, four-bedroom Meyerland area home was nothing like Leela remembered. Visible repairs were needed, and the lawn was overgrown and neglected.

"Pah-pah. Why do you want to come by here?" Leela asked.

It had been a month since she'd defied her mother and checked in on her grandfather. He now called a senior apartment complex home, but he still wanted her to pass by the house he once owned.

"I was so proud when we found that house. Your grandmother was on top of the world. This was one of Houston's original uppity neighborhoods," he boasted.

Leela looked around at the aging houses and marveled at how plain and simple they looked.

"Now, it ain't nothing compared to that mini-mansion you and Riley gots, but it was the first thing me and your grands ever owned outright. I worked hard to pay off that mortgage. Wheew! Them was the days for sure," he said.

"Pah-pah. Let's go," Leela whined.

"I just don't like living up in that building. It's like e'erybody always up in ya' business. You can't get a moment of peace. Then, they wanna be tryin' to tell you who can come and go in ya own place," he said.

"Pah-pah. The lady at the front desk is quite nice. When she realized I was your granddaughter, she pulled me to the side and asked me to explain the rules so you'd understand. You have to let the maids in to clean the place. That's part of the perks of living there."

"Rubbish!" he spat. "Let's go. But I wanna go to Golden Corral or Luby's. I'm not ready to go back there."

Leela pulled away from the curb and drove out of the subdivision where her grandparents once lived. For a long while, her grandfather didn't speak. She could tell he was deep in thought and she felt sorry for him.

"You wanna tell me what happened?" she asked softly.

"Ah. It ain't nothin'," he said and swatted the air in front of him.

"It *is* something, Pah-pah. But we don't have to talk about it now if you don't want to."

"Your mama still mad at me, hmm?" he asked.

Leela nodded. She didn't want to get into a conversation about her mother because she didn't want to think about all the awful things her mother had said.

"We can go grab lunch, but if we do, you have to promise to tell me what I want to know," Leela said.

Her grandfather turned to look at her. "What is it you wanna know?"

"I wanna know who you got living up in your apartment with you. And I wanna know how your finances are going," Leela said.

Her grandfather frowned and mumbled something under his breath. He tugged on the strap of the seat belt that crossed his chest.

"So, what's it gonna be? Are we going to Luby's or Corral?" she asked. "Or, are you going back to your apartment?"

"Why can't we just enjoy a nice quiet lunch?" he asked.

Leela wasn't about to back down. She felt like there was no other way to get to the bottom of what was going on with her grandfather.

"It's simple really; if we go to lunch, we talk. If you don't want to talk, we go back to your apartment," she said.

"Ain't no doggone apartment; might as well be a prison for old folks."

A few minutes later, he added, "I'd rather Golden Corral over Luby's."

There was a part of Riley that agreed with what Bill was saying. But he couldn't tell his friend about the agreement he had made with his wife.

Over the last four weeks, Leela and Riley agreed to avoid spending too much time with their two newly single, best friends. Samantha was now wild and loose as far as Riley was concerned, and Bill was like a lovesick stalker.

"Now, what's this no-spouse party thing again?" Riley asked.

The little voice that warned him to beware had lost out to his curiosity. Besides, he could use some time away from his spouse since she didn't want to act right.

"C'mon, Bruh. Don't talk yourself out of it. All you need to know is there are no spouses allowed. Just think about it like a place where you can go chill with some other dudes and a few females. It's really just a little get-together with a theme," Bill said. "And let's not forget, the old ball-and-chain has had you on lock for a good two months now."

Riley ignored his overexaggeration. He didn't expect Leela back until late because she was spending time with her grandfather, and the old man was so lonely, he hated her to leave.

"I ain't looking for no drama, Bill," Riley warned.

"C'mon, Dawg. Give me more credit than that. I'm telling you. It's a little get-together and I think you'll like it. What's up? Now you can't hang with your boys anymore? You ain't been out in weeks, Man."

Bill had a point there. Riley had to admit he missed being out with his friend, and he knew for sure, there was no one who could get him to do something he didn't want to do. How much harm was there in hanging out with the guys? Besides, he ran things in his house anyway. Lately, he'd been laying low and he and Leela had been up under each other for the last month like they were glued to one another.

"Where is it, and what time?" Riley asked.

"Oh, it's out there in my old neighborhood. A nice place over there, trust me, Dude. You're gonna like this," Bill said.

Against his better judgment, Riley told himself there couldn't be much harm in going to a little house party. It had been ages since he'd attended one.

"So what's up, Dawg?" Bill asked.

"I'll let you know."

He had already decided to go, but he wanted to let Bill sweat it out a bit.

"C'mon, Dawg. What, you need me to talk to Leela for you?" Bill asked.

"Oh, I see you got jokes, huh? You know I'm good when it comes to that."

"Oh, no jokes, but if she's riding you hard, just say so and I'll back off. I ain't trying to cause problems over there in paradise. I just wanna hang for a few hours with my dawg. That ain't against the law, is it?"

"Where's this house?" Riley asked.

"So, you coming?"

"Yeah, Man. Give me the address."

"Hell. I'll do one better. I'ma come scoop you. You can't beat that, hmm?"

"You ain't gotta do that," Riley protested.

"Nah. I want to. C'mon. We got some catching up to do. Anyway, I wanna hear all about that plan we discussed, so I'll be by around nine."

CHAPTER 12

The no-spouse party was going down in a home two blocks away from Bill and Samantha's old house. Bill maneuvered his car through the winding, tree-lined streets and multi-million-dollar homes.

"You been back here since ya'll sold the house?" Riley asked.

"I came back a couple weeks ago. Actually it was to one of these parties. Man, I'm telling you, when I was there, I was, like, how come nobody ever told me about this before now?" Bill said.

Riley ignored the wicked smirk on his friend's face. He gazed out the window at the spectacular homes that were brightly lit with what looked like spotlights.

Minutes later, after they parked, Riley followed Bill into a side door that led into a spectacular kitchen. Red and blue hues rained down over the appliances that blended into dark cherrywood cabinetry. Several half-naked women assembled near snacks spread across a large granite slab that served as an island. Several men hovered nearby.

"Tight, huh?" Bill leaned in to whisper to Riley.

As Riley strolled in and took in the scene, soft suggestive reggae sounds filled the air.

"Wanna go out there?" Bill asked. He motioned ahead toward the backyard.

Riley turned to see a DJ who was spinning on two turntables set up next to the pool. On the wooden deck, several couples were in the bubbling Jacuzzi. The scene was close to paradise.

"Yeah. That's what's up," Riley said as he looked around. The setting was laid-back and everyone seemed to be having a great time.

"You ain't seen nothing yet, Dawg," Bill said.

Riley was hyped over the scene that played out before him, but despite how hard he tried, he couldn't help but wonder what he would do if Kelly walked in or was outside. He hoped his friend had gotten over a woman who had clearly moved on.

As they stepped out onto the deck, Riley suddenly stopped at the sight of a shapely woman who cradled a beer bottle between her hands. The seductive smile that stretched across her face was familiar.

Her smile was once the equivalent to kryptonite. Riley grinned hard. Every man had one of those, that one woman who threatened to send him back to his boyhood days because he'd follow her like he had no mind of his own.

"OhmyGod! You came," she squealed.

"Natasha? What you doing here?" Riley asked. His voice shook a bit as he spoke. It wasn't that he was nervous or weak; those days were long gone. He was pleasantly surprised.

Natasha wore a fitted crop top with a matching pencil skirt that looked like she was made to wear it. The top had a large key hole that showed off her ample breasts. Her short, jet-black, feathered haircut framed her caramel-colored, oval-shaped face perfectly.

Although she looked like the typical almond brown-eyed beauty, the power she once held over Riley was like a rare form of voodoo. She was the master at seduction and mind games, with a knack for making men do what she wanted. Riley was glad to be away from her. Leela was a safer and less threatening alternative and he was happy he had survived Natasha. He had searched high and low for a woman with less sex appeal and one whom he controlled versus the other way around. Leela was that woman, and after what Riley considered the right amount of time, he married her to make sure he'd always maintain the upper hand.

Bill stood off to the side and abruptly went quiet.

Natasha released a soft sigh. "Bill didn't tell you?" she asked.

Riley looked around in confusion. Bill smiled wickedly.

"Dawg. If I woulda told you everything, you know you would've found a way to back out," he said.

"You mean you didn't tell him why he's here?" Natasha asked.

Riley didn't know whether he should sock Bill or hug Natasha. It was a struggle, but he fought the urge.

"It was me." Natasha smiled. "I'm the one who requested your presence at this no-spouse party," she said sweetly.

Leela held her breath for as long as she could. The stench that filled the space around her, burned her nostrils and made her eyes water. She pinched her nose and stepped cautiously.

"I thought they had maid service in here," she said.

"They do, but I don't need no strangers going through all my personal stuff," her grandfather said.

"Pah-pah. It smells rank in here. Nobody is gonna be going through your stuff..."

Leela's voice trailed off when she thought she heard shuffling sounds coming from the back. Her eyes caught at the sight of the sofa turned into a makeshift bed. The place was a mess. Food containers and empty beer bottles and cans were strewn all over.

"So, you won't let the maids in, but you don't clean up, either, Pah-pah?"

"Aw, Leela. Your grandmother used to handle all of that."

"Yes. But she's not here. You're by yourself now; you can't live like this. It's a pigsty in here," Leela complained.

Suddenly, the bedroom door creaked open and a half-dressed boy-man strolled out scratching his stomach beneath a dingy wife-beater undershirt.

"What up out here, old man?" the boy said.

He seemed surprised when his eyes focused on Leela, but just as quickly, he boldly scanned her up and down. "Oh. S'up, Leela?"

Unable to control her emotions, Leela's face contorted into a nasty frown.

"Darnell?" She hadn't laid eyes on Rhonda's oldest child in years.

"Oh. Pops. You ain't told Leela I'm crashing here witchu for a minute?"

Leela looked at her grandfather and noticed something she'd never seen before. Her grandfather cowered.

Sudden alarm fanned through Leela as she reevaluated the scene. When had her grandfather ever drunk alcohol? The food containers were Chinese food boxes and bags from Jack in the Box and McDonald's. She couldn't remember a time when her grandfather ate fast-food like that.

"So you sitting up in here mooching off my grandfather, sleeping on his couch and drinking beer all damn day long?!" Leela yelled at Darnell. She couldn't contain her anger.

"Yo. I ain't never liked you or your mama. Y'all always thought y'all was better than my moms and us. I'm glad he finally man-upped and told y'all what was what."

"Get the hell out! Get your trifling, wannabe gangbanging, loser ass up outta here before I call the police!" Leela shouted.

Darnell rubbed his belly some more and chuckled like he was mocking her.

"Yo. This here ain't none of your business. You don't even know what the hell you talking about. You can't call the cops on me! For what? I ain't trespassing. I live here. Like I told you, my pops let me and Danisha chill here for a minute! So, call the cops all you want. What they gon' do?" He shrugged.

Leela turned her rage to her grandfather.

"Don't you see they're using you? You're worried about the maids going through your stuff? We've been gone all day and half the night. We come back here and where is he? He's all up in your bedroom, Pah-pah. How come you're not worried about what he was doing back there?"

"His bedroom?" Darnell laughed. "See. I told you. You don't know shit. Pops sleeps right there on the couch. Me and Danisha share the room," he boasted.

"Wow! And you're proud of that." Leela shook her head. "It's too much!" Leela was so mad, she shook visibly. "You ain't got no shame, that you let an old man sleep on the friggin' couch while you take his bed?"

Darnell belched loudly. He didn't cover his mouth, nor did he excuse his behavior.

"Yo, he used to roughin' it. Me? Not so much. I ain't made to sleep on a couch and shit like that. What they say? These old cats can handle all of that and then some. Ain't that right, Pops?!"

Leela was so enraged! She struggled to keep her hands to herself.

CHAPTER 13

Natasha looked better than Riley remembered and her divine scent was just as intoxicating as it had always been. He had a thing for the scent of a woman. He appreciated women who went the extra mile in that department. He suspected that was something Natasha had never forgotten.

Despite all of her faults, she made sure she appealed to all of his senses. And her efforts didn't go unnoticed.

"Damn you, Bill!" She shook her head in exasperation.

Riley closed his eyes and pulled in a deep breath. Her voice—Natasha was passionate and was never afraid to express herself. She sauntered in Bill's direction, and Riley's eyes followed her every move. There was something alluring and sexy about her, even after all these years.

"I told you to talk to him about it and if he didn't want to come, not to bring him," she said to Bill.

Bill shifted his weight from one side to the next as he kept a nervous eye on the five-foot-five bombshell in front of him.

"Look, I know my boy. I knew what I had to do to get him here. So either you gonna stand over here and fuss at me, or you gonna go over there and make the best of the limited time you got with him," he said.

Natasha quickly masked her disdain before she shifted her gaze back to Riley. Reluctantly, she moved away from Bill and closer to

Riley. The smile that made its way to her face was genuine. But it was clear that her focus had switched and moved to Riley.

"I know your situation. But that's what makes a no-spouse party so unique." She looked downward momentarily. "You see, this is where people gather and invite the one that got away."

"Oooh. Hence the no-spouse meaning," Riley said with a slight chuckle.

Riley thought it was simply a party where married people attended without their spouse. He looked at the people in the Jacuzzi and had a different impression now that he knew a few could be married and were simply taking a break from their spouse.

"Soooo. It's by invitation only, and how it's supposed to work is, an ex reaches out and invites you to come. It's sort of an understanding where just about anything goes, and the beauty of it is, nothing leaves this house. You don't have to worry about your business getting back to your spouse."

Riley's eyes grew wide in surprise. For the first time, the smile seemed to slip from Natasha's face.

"I mean, you don't have to do anything you don't want to do," she quickly added.

Natasha looked around and moved a bit closer to Riley. "Actually, do you want to go somewhere a little more private? Just so we can talk. I mean, there are a few things I want to share with you," she said. "I'm sure discretion is important to you."

Bill was gone. It was all on Riley, and he knew that his next move would be that, his alone. It wasn't like Natasha asked to screw him; she just wanted to go somewhere quiet and talk. But the outfit she wore screamed, "Anything goes!"

"I'm sorry Bill didn't tell you what was up. But I hope that doesn't mean you're not happy to see me."

With each step Riley took down the dark, carpeted hallway, he knew he was wrong. But it was as if he had lost all sense of right and wrong.

They arrived at a bedroom door and Natasha eased up against it. After she listened for a second, she knocked softly. When no one answered, she twisted the knob and pushed the door open.

"C'mon." She beckoned Riley with a single crooked finger. "Sssh. Don't worry, I won't tell a soul. It's our little secret, okay?"

He couldn't not follow her. She had gone through so much to bring him to the party; the least he could do was go and hear her out.

Inside the master bedroom, Riley released a massive sigh of relief when Natasha continued past the custom-made bed, mirrored walls, and stopped at a set of balcony doors. He told himself maybe she really only wanted to talk. After all, it had been years, so it was only right that they needed time to catch up.

They walked out into the starry night, and Riley once again told himself she only wanted to talk. The setting was perfect. The balcony was in a secluded part of the house, so it overlooked bushes and a lake. They were close enough to the action to hear what was going on, and enjoy the music, but not so close that anyone would notice them. It was all good since they were only going to talk; besides, he wore the pants any damn way. There was no reason for him to fear Natasha, Leela, or any other woman; he was the man.

"I told your ass to stay away from him! If you would listen, you would've known he had them illegitimate bastards living up in there with him. I don't care what they do to his old simple behind," Linda complained.

"But they've got him sleeping on the couch! And you should smell the place. It's awful. It's a mess and I felt so bad for him."

"I don't know why. Look at what that bastard did to Big Mama. I don't feel the least bit of sympathy for his ass. Let him suffer over there with them."

Leela suddenly regretted calling her mother. She wondered whether her mother's heart would ever soften when it came to her grandfather.

Usually, Linda had the answer or solution to most problems. She was the family member who never hesitated to act, and her action always garnered results.

Leela listened as her mother went on and on about her grandfather and what a loser he was. By the time Leela pulled up to her subdivision, she was glad she was finally close to home.

"Mama, I need to go," Leela said.

"Okay. But don't say nothing to Big Mama. I don't want her getting all worked up over this or anything else dealing with him."

Leela thought she felt bad as she left her grandfather's house, but by the time she'd finally gotten off the phone with her mother, she felt worse.

She called for Riley when she got in, but couldn't find him anywhere. They'd agreed that neither would go out without the other, so she wasn't concerned that he may be out with Bill. Maybe he'd just taken a late run.

Thoughts about her husband's whereabouts made Leela think about Samantha. If she was honest with herself, she missed being with her. It didn't matter who Samantha had become, Leela still enjoyed the time they'd spent together. There was something about Samantha's new-found freedom that left Leela yearning.

It didn't matter that the difference between married Samantha and single Samantha was incredible. Leela knew she could get used to it. She quickly shook those thoughts from her mind and stripped naked to take a shower.

She figured Riley should be back by the time she was done.

An hour and a half after a hot shower and several glasses of wine later, Leela considered calling area hospitals. She had tried Riley's cell phone several times, but got his voicemail. She contemplated calling the police. What if he had been mugged?

Finally, she went to bed, but at 2:45 a.m. when Leela rolled over and realized the space next to her was crisp and cold, she began to panic.

"Something must be wrong," she said aloud.

Pulling herself upright, she looked around the room and decided he must be downstairs in his man-room. That had to be it. There was no way Riley would be out so late after they had reached an agreement about what needed to be done to keep their marriage intact.

Drowsily, Leela pulled herself up from the bed and padded down the hall and down the stairs. She passed the front door, and walked down the long hallway that led to the rear and lower part of their house.

From a distance, she could tell her husband wasn't in his man-cave.

Now Leela was pissed for sure. He had to be out with Bill; she felt it. There was nothing she could do at that hour, but she was pissed.

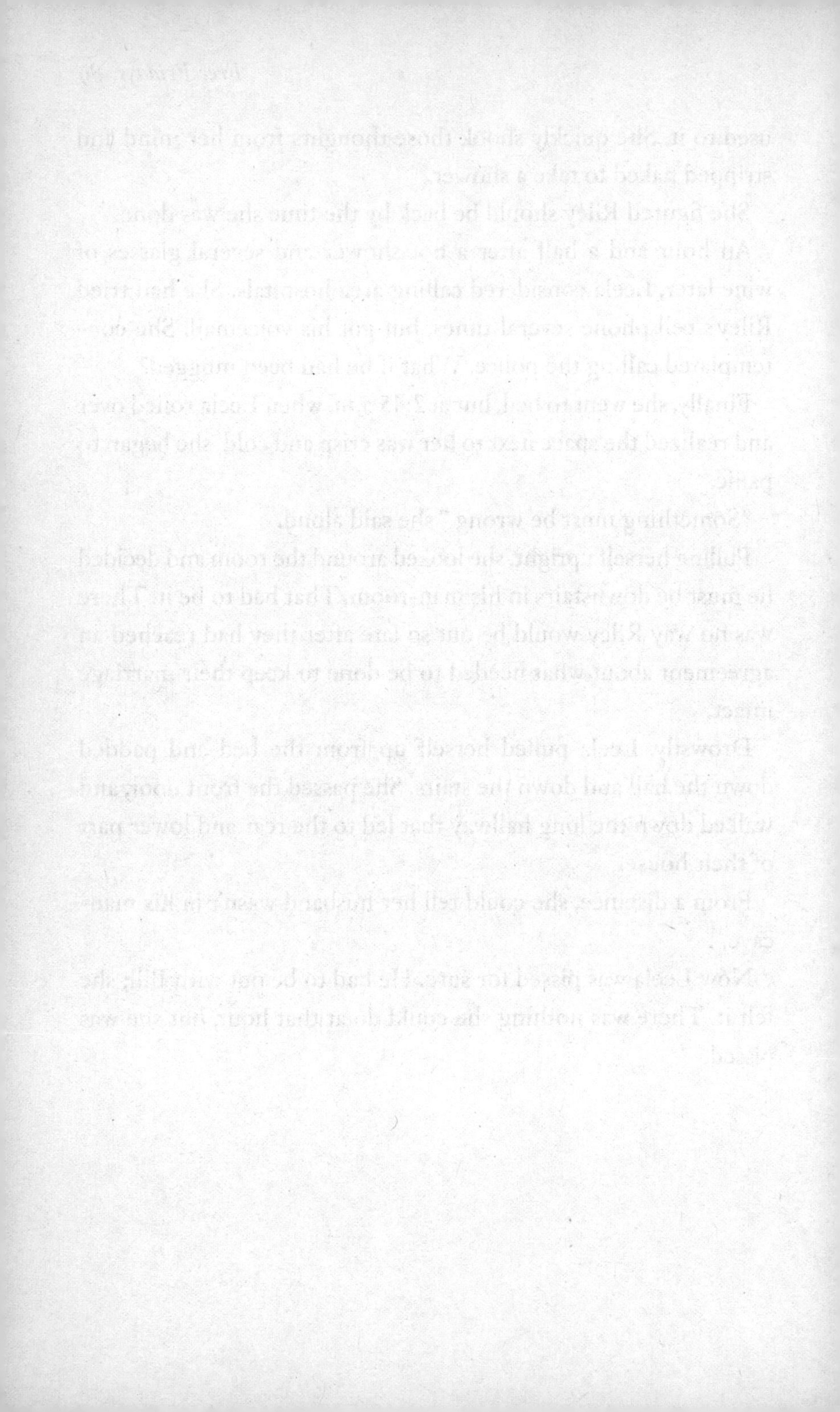

CHAPTER 14

Two weeks after Leela was certain Riley had backtracked on his word, she was still a bit salty. But she had held her tongue and fought the urge to complain because she had plans of her own. First, she needed to convince her mother that both Big Mama and Pah-pah needed help. She knew Linda didn't want to help her father, but there was no way they could abandon him; it wouldn't be right.

Normally, she'd discuss her plans with Riley and try to figure out what to do, but lately, she felt like he was slipping once again.

Next, she needed to reach out to her girl and make some plans. It made no sense that she was the only person who honored the rules. Riley had the nerve to come home like nothing had happened. Leela didn't ride him over it, but mentally she told herself, one good turn deserved another. Why should she avoid Samantha if he was still running around with Bill?

"Hey, Babe, I'll be late tonight. Office happy hour or something like that," Riley said.

His comment broke her train of thought. Leela looked at her husband side-eyed but didn't say a cross word. She knew that was his way of saying he was going out to drink with Bill after work. She liked how his rules were only for her to follow and for him to disregard when the feeling hit him.

"Okay, how late you think you'll be?" she asked.

Riley stopped, but he didn't turn to face her. "I'll call you if it's too late."

Without another word, he was out the door.

Leela felt so alone. It wasn't just his absence, but lately, she'd felt like he wasn't completely there with her. Something had gotten ahold of her husband, and she didn't know what to do about it.

Her problems were big, but she knew the issue with Pah-pah and Big Mama was even bigger. The biggest issue was the fact that her mother wanted to be oblivious to what her father was going through. It was clear that Linda had chosen Big Mama's side, and while Leela understood, she had to figure out a way to prevent Linda from completely banishing her grandfather.

When the phone rang and it was Samantha, Leela didn't think twice about picking up.

"Hey, you!" she squealed into the phone. Leela was happy to hear from Samantha. Guilt washed over Leela temporarily because she had taken the pact with her husband seriously despite the fact that he hadn't.

"It's about damn time. I don't know who I pissed off," Samantha began. "But this shit has got to stop. I ain't seen your pretty ass in nearly three months, and it ain't right! It ain't right, I tell you!"

Leela laughed so hard she nearly squirted. She could tell Samantha had been drinking, but she didn't care. Actually, she felt even more slighted. If she had gone to Happy Hour with Samantha, maybe she'd be feeling good too.

"You are truly special," Leela said into the phone.

"When are we getting together? I'm sick and tired of this dry spell. I know I brought you home drunk the last time, but I've been punished enough! Enough already. Who do I have to blow for a night with my bestie?"

Leela loved Samantha's energy and figured it wouldn't hurt to spend some time with her girl. Besides, she knew her husband was off somewhere with Bill.

"Maybe we can do Happy Hour this week or something," Leela said.

"You promise?" Samantha asked.

"Yeah. I've been swamped with Pah-pah and so much. I could use some time for myself," Leela admitted.

"I'm gonna plan something for us. Nothing too extravagant, but just something for us to relax and relieve some stress. I don't want to piss Riley off again. So you just tell me what day next week is best for you. If you can't do Happy Hour, maybe we can do a spa day or something. Just let me know."

"Okay. I will," Leela said. As she was about to hang up, Samantha yelled.

"I'm giving you two days! If I don't hear from you, I'm coming over there and it won't be pretty," Samantha quipped. "You know Riley don't like me anymore, so don't let it come to that; hear me?"

"I hear you."

The call cheered her up. But more importantly, it made Leela see that her husband was a hypocrite. There was no telling how long he'd been hanging with Bill despite the fact that they were supposed to stay clear of Bill and Samantha.

Leela knew her husband felt like she should follow his rules because he was the man of the house, but she had news for him. She was getting fed up with his crap. And the last thing any man wanted was a woman who was fed up.

Riley shoved the food into his mouth like he wasn't sure when he'd eat again. His mind was all over the place. When he was at home with Leela, he couldn't stop thinking about Natasha.

That was one of the main reasons he didn't want to be bothered with Natasha again. She made him weak. There was just something about a woman who didn't mind doing anything she thought her man wanted. Back in the day, Natasha would fuck, or suck, on demand, no questions asked. He couldn't think of a time when Leela had been so willing.

He knew his wife was dealing with a lot. He understood that the problem with her grandparents had taken a toll on her, but he had issues of his own.

Weeks had passed since they had shared a kiss or had sex and she seemed to be fine. What was up with that? It was a wife's duty to make sure her man was satisfied at all times, and she knew how strongly he felt about that. Perhaps his wife was getting hers elsewhere, and that meant she no longer cared about him and his sexual needs.

"I take it you like your breakfast," Leela said.

He had barely looked up from his plate. "Yeah. It's good." Once he finished eating, he pushed back from the table and looked over at Leela. "That was great, Babe. I'm about to go hop in the shower."

Lately, their conversations were limited to talks over meals or brief greetings in passing.

Before he walked into the bathroom, he wondered how long he'd survive. He needed to do something because he was desperate. Riley walked into the bathroom and turned on the shower. He put his favorite playlist on repeat and told himself he knew he needed to do the right thing.

But his mind wouldn't cooperate. The minute the music took ahold of him, his mind went back to Natasha and the party. There they were on the balcony, beneath a blanket of stars with some of the most suggestive reggae songs playing in the background.

When Lady Saw's "Heels On" blared through the air, Natasha was transformed.

When she'd looked at him, her eyes were ablaze with lust.

She sang the lyrics in such a seductive way, Riley felt himself go weak. "Let me fuck you with my heels on," she sang. "I wanna fuck you like I own ya'."

Riley had closed his eyes. He'd felt himself slipping and struggled to resist the feeling. But it seemed the more he refused to give in, the stronger Natasha came on.

He could smell the hint of alcohol on her breath when she'd invaded his personal space. Riley had stood transfixed for a few moments as she'd moved in. He didn't try to stop her when she'd grabbed his crotch and stroked him. Natasha always knew how to send his blood boiling, and it seemed time had done nothing to lessen the power she once had over him.

In one swift move, she'd locked eyes with him, unzipped his fly and lowered herself to her knees. Riley had shivered with raw excitement as Natasha took him into her mouth. That was something Leela rarely did.

Riley had staggered back slightly; the space spun, and whirled out of control. With each move, Natasha had clung desperately to him. Riley had grabbed the railing to steady himself; his legs felt like they were made of cloth and he could barely stand.

The sound of Leela walking into the bathroom brought him back from that memory.

It was Leela placing a stack of towels into the armoire. She glanced at him.

"You wanna come in and join me? The water feels great."

"Some of us have work to do around here," she chided as she walked out of the bathroom.

Riley was relieved once the door closed. Now if only he could keep his mind focused on his marriage and not his ex, he might have a chance.

CHAPTER 15

Leela knew for sure her life was falling apart. It all started with the text message she saw on Riley's phone. The message was simple. It said: *next time we need to go all the way!* It had a few hearts and lipstick characters in front of a hashtag that read *no spouse parties rock!*

As she waited for Samantha at the Wine Dive in midtown, she kept going over the message and what it could've meant. She had no idea who had sent it because the name attached to it was only two initials.

"You're in such deep thought over here. I waved at you from the door and it was like you looked right through me," Samantha said as she slid into a chair across from Leela.

"I'm sorry. I've got so much going on these days. I've gotta figure out a way to get these people out of my grandfather's house, and at home—" Leela stopped speaking abruptly.

Samantha's face twisted in confusion. "And at home what?" she asked.

"What's a 'no-spouse' party?" Leela suddenly asked.

A wicked grin stretched across Samantha's face and mischief danced in her eyes. "Why you ask?" Samantha leaned in close. "This guy I went out with a few weeks ago told me about it. Oooh, did someone invite you to one? I think it started up on social media sites, but I was like, it's a pretty cool idea."

"What is it?" Leela asked. She couldn't hide the irritation in her voice. "I mean, I've heard of companies that have a no-spouse rule for their holiday parties, but we're nowhere close to the holidays."

"Girl, it's a party where someone from your past invites you to come without your spouse so y'all can hook up," Samantha said. When her eyes looked away, Leela could tell Samantha's level of interest had wavered since she didn't know what the party was all about.

"Like, to cheat?" Leela asked. Her stomach felt like it was tied in a dozen knots. Worry invaded her features. Only then did Samantha's focus return to her.

"Oh, wait a minute. Not you, did somebody invite Riley to one?" Samantha pursed her lips and leaned back a bit. "Umph."

"So, you're trying to tell me people invite their exes to a party so they can cheat? What kind of foolishness is that?"

"I'm trying to tell you, Leela. Marriage ain't what it used to be. Honey, if you ask me, soon, we're gonna see people start to change the definition of what's considered a successful marriage."

Leela frowned. "What do you mean?"

"Who says you have to be married 'til death do you part?"

"Uh, your vows; God," Leela answered.

"Do you know how many people are not religious these days? Think how marriage has changed over time. People get married in a drive-through window or they go downtown. Same sex marriages are now legal. And people have already altered vows to pick and choose what they want to include. When was the last time you heard a woman say she'd obey her husband?"

"And what does all of that have to do with anything?" Leela asked. She had already started to dismiss Samantha and whatever point she was trying to make.

"No, hear me out. All I'm saying is this. Just because a marriage ends in divorce, it doesn't mean it wasn't successful. I'm not talking about Big Mama and your grandfather. I still don't get that one; after fifty-two years, y'all should just hang in there. But what I'm talking about is cases where after five, maybe seven or even ten years, the couple has developed into different people and maybe want different things out of life. Why shouldn't they go their separate ways and call it a day?" Samantha put up her hand to stop Leela from interjecting. "Besides, once sex hits the A-B-C stage, it's really time to do something different."

Leela's eyebrows bunched together as she listened to Samantha. It was obvious Samantha had given this lots of thought.

"You know, ABC sex, where you only do it on anniversaries, birthdays and Christmas!" Samantha said. "Of course, none of this applies if you have kids; that would complicate things. But if it's just two adults who still have some love for each other, but they feel they've done all they could together, it seems very appropriate to me that they should be able to move on," she added. "The thrill is gone; the challenge no longer exists; and they've stunted each other's growth. Why stick it out?"

"Umm. Yeeaaah, what you're talking about, that's called dating," Leela said.

Samantha rolled her eyes and picked up her menu. "Closed minds stay stuck," she muttered.

"I'm far from close-minded," Leela defended. "But call me what you want. When I took those vows, I didn't take them for five, seven or ten years, and I took them knowing that this was the man I wanted to spend the rest of my life with. What's the point if you can just switch every five years?" Leela looked down at her nail bed. "Besides, I put up with a lot. All wives do. Do you know how many nights I don't get a wink of sleep? It's three in the freakin' morning and Ry gets a bad case of restless dick syndrome!" Leela rolled her eyes dramatically. "It's exhausting, but it is what it is; you do what you gotta do, until there's a pill for that!"

Following Samantha's lead, Leela picked up her own menu. Her mind was supposed to be focused on food and drink choices, but it was stuck on the "no spouse" party and Samantha's suggestion for how the institution of marriage needed to be updated to fit the times and a restless generation.

"I have a very open mind," Leela huffed.

"You are missing my point."

"No. I think you've explained it very well. You want to change the institution of marriage and turn it into registered dating."

"That's not what I said. And I don't have to explain it to you. But look all around you, Leela. Marriage is not what it used to be. We continue to evolve as a people. We change as we evolve. Why do I have to be considered a failure because I've outgrown my spouse? Why can't I simply find someone else who shares my new interests? Or better yet, why can't I have sex with another man who turns me on? I think people are afraid to publically embrace what I'm saying, but in private, or even when they're among like-minded people, their actions prove they agree."

Leela had moved on. She didn't even respond as she perused the menu for possible options. But, as she prepared for dinner with Samantha, there was no way she could have known just how soon she'd be put to the test.

The splash of cold water woke his senses and felt good against his skin, but nothing could really fix what was wrong. The reflection that stared back at him in the mirror was one of a man he hardly recognized.

Riddled with guilt, Riley told himself he needed to move on emotionally. He was a man after all, and a real man is built to handle the difficult and meet challenges head-on. He hadn't responded to any of the suggestive text messages from Natasha and when she sent him an MP3 of the song *Heels On* by Lady Saw, he purposely didn't listen to it, at first.

Startled at the sound of her voice, Riley jumped at the question.

"That's an interesting song, the lyrics," Leela said as she leaned against the sink. "Where'd you hear it?"

Riley's eyebrows elevated slightly. He used a fluffy hand towel to dry his face. "Oh, that?"

"Yeah, I've never heard it before. Kinda raunchy if you ask me," Leela said. "I can't even picture you listening to music like that," Leela added, wrinkling her nose.

"Music like what? Reggae?"

Riley knew he needed to play it cool. What did she care which songs he listened to during his alone time? What the hell was she doing in the bathroom while he showered anyway?

"We haven't listened to Reggae since our trip to Jamaica, or was it the Bahamas? Either way, it's just odd to hear you listening to this. And, the lyrics are so graphic. They're just not you."

Riley struggled to hide his frustration. He raised his right arm and ran the stick of deodorant under it. The lyrics were him more than ever. He tried to tell himself it wasn't fair that he was looking for a reason to find something wrong with Leela.

A sense of relief washed over him when the song went off. It looked like his wife was about to leave. Then suddenly, she turned and said, "Another graphic song? What's up with you lately?"

"Nothing. What are you talking about? Damn! It's music," Riley snapped.

The look Leela gave him made him think she suspected there was more to it, but he knew his wife well enough to know she didn't want to go there with him.

When Leela walked out of the bathroom, he felt relieved. She had no business questioning him about his music, or anything else for that matter. What difference did it make which music he chose to listen to?

Natasha would like the song. She was different from Leela. Natasha liked what he liked, she did what he said, and if she thought it would make him happy, she'd do it. No one was perfect. Just like Leela, Natasha had her faults, but more and more, Riley felt her open-minded approach to anything he wanted, had Leela beat—hands down.

Leela wasn't too headstrong, but there were times when she behaved like she had forgotten that he was in charge and that what he said was the rule of the house.

In the beginning, he loved the fact that Leela looked up to him and always looked to him for the right answer. He wanted his wife to feel like she could count on him.

Lately, she'd been working his nerves. He was frustrated, and her constant nagging didn't help. Riley released a heavy breath when she finally walked out of the bathroom for good.

He continued to listen to his music and think about everything he should've done with Natasha.

Dressed and ready to go, he stopped and looked at his reflection one last time. As he caught a final glimpse of himself, he decided it was time to present the idea to Leela.

He still loved her; he wanted their marriage to work, but he knew that unless they took action, unless they did something drastic, they were headed for disaster. After all, he was already flirting with it.

CHAPTER 16

Leela's eyes held a hint of alarm. She struggled to contain the sheer disgust and fury that was brewing deep inside and threatening to explode into all-out rage. Her husband must've fallen somewhere and bumped his head really hard.

As she listened, she blinked a few times and bit down on her bottom lip. What she really wanted to do was go upside her husband's head and knock some good sense into his ignorant behind. One good hard blow; that would do the trick.

"Are you guys doing okay over here?" The waitress smiled as she looked down on them. Leela didn't even notice as she approached. One minute her husband's words were flapping around in her head like trapped birds struggling to get out of a cage; the next the waitress was at the table.

"Yeah. We're good," Riley quickly said.

"Okay, well, your food will be here soon, and I'll be back to check on you guys." She smiled, shook her strawberry-colored hair, then turned and walked toward another table.

"Think about what I'm saying," Riley said, the moment they were alone again. "It's the only way we're gonna make it." He stared at her.

Leela listened carefully to everything he said and did her best to push away the heavy feeling in her heart. There was no way she could hit him in public; there would be many witnesses. Domestic violence charges worked both ways now.

She didn't realize he was finished with his plan until he sat wide-eyed and waited. His expression was anxious.

"Just so I understand you," Leela began, "you want me to agree to an open marriage?" Her arched eyebrows crawled up her forehead. "And so that means we're still married, because that's what you want. But you also want to be able to screw other women. And let me guess, this all came to you after you met with one of those women at a no-spouse party, and you two hooked up. And I suppose the trip down memory lane was so good, that she's decided she wanted to keep seeing you? So, the two of you put your heads together and finally figured out a way to allow you to have both me and her. Now you bring me to this fancy restaurant to roll out your new plan like I'm supposed to get up and give you a round of applause?"

Leela was so pissed, she wanted to douse Riley with every liquid she could find, then flip the table over so it would land on top of him. Thereafter, she'd strut out of there.

"Leela, you serious? Why you trippin' right now?" Riley asked. He glanced around the crowded restaurant. "I thought you agreed to have an open mind."

She chuckled and stared at him for a second. "Then after all of that, you ask me whether I'm serious? Like I'm the one with the fucking problem? You ask whether I'm serious?" she huffed.

Riley looked around the restaurant again, this time more nervously than before. The only thing he hated more than PDA was people who argued or fought in public. He couldn't believe his wife was about to behave like some untrained ghetto girl.

"You really thought that shit was gonna fly with me?" she asked through tight lips.

Leela noticed his left eye begin to twitch, but she refused to let up. "Oh, and this new arrangement of yours, am I able to fuck anyone I want, too, or just you? I mean, I need to know *all* the rules," she spat out.

"You really need to check yourself right now," Riley warned. His face was void of any expression when he spoke. He hoped she was picking up on clues designed to help her. She knew good and well that he didn't play this kind of game.

Leela frowned. "You cannot be serious." She shook her head in sheer disgust. "I can't believe this was your brilliant idea on how we can pump fresh new energy into our marriage," Leela said. "And I need to check *myself?*" she asked. Her voice was laced with repulsion. She used a finger to stab at her own chest as she emphasized the words that flew from her mouth.

Riley cleared his throat. His eyes darted from the left to the right, and he took in their surroundings. From what he could tell, no one was concerned about the near-ruckus that was unfolding at his table. He looked at his wife like he really didn't understand her reaction.

Suddenly, the waitress was back. "Okay, I just checked and your food should be here in the next ten minutes."

"Can we get it to go instead?" Leela asked.

Riley never looked at the waitress.

"To go? Is everything okay? I know it seems like it's taking a bit longer—" The waitress's green eyes expanded to double their size.

"It's not that. We just, something came up and we need to go," Leela said.

The waitress looked back and forth between her and Riley. She seemed very disappointed about the change in plans. She leaned in closer to Leela, "Listen. I'm real sorry about all of this. I could see if my manager would be willing to knock something off the price. You know, because of the wait," she offered.

Leela raised a hand to stop her. "Seriously, it's okay. We really do need to go. Thank you for the offer, but we'll just take it to go; it's no big deal."

Reluctantly, the waitress turned, and left without another word.

"Leela, I'm not talking about a free for all. I'm not even suggesting an open marriage."

"Then what were you thinking?" she asked. Leela could hardly mask her disdain as she looked at him. She noticed everything: his occasional eye twitch, his stone-faced stare that she figured were supposed to make her scared and back down. The man was more of a fool than she'd realized.

"I was thinking maybe one Friday out of each month, we get a free pass to do whatever. Maybe you want to go hang out with your girl and not constantly have to worry about getting back home. I'm not thinking about my wife screwing another man; that's not where I was going with this. It's one day out of a month for freedom. We can do something different together, or we can do something apart. No questions asked, no strings attached, no worry, no fuss. It ain't like I'm trying to go be with another woman. I guess I'm looking around at marriages that keep falling apart, and I don't want it to happen to us; that's it. Don't give it another thought. I don't want you doing anything that makes you uncomfortable. That's not what the idea was all about," he said.

The way his wife looked at him made Riley very uncomfortable. He was still the man of their house and the truth of the matter was, if he thought something was good for their marriage or their household, she was supposed to be on board, few if any questions asked, period.

He'd let her have her moment. All the loud talking, swiveling her neck and shit she knew he'd never stand for, was becoming a bit much, but he'd give her a pass—this time.

Later, at home, Leela paid close attention to the way she and Riley moved around the house. She had lost her appetite, but Riley wanted to eat his food.

"I'm gonna take it downstairs. I wanna watch the game," he said. He behaved like nothing had happened.

"Okay. Cool. I could use a relaxing bath," Leela commented. As her husband prepared to walk out of the kitchen with his dinner from the restaurant, he stopped and turned to her.

"Listen, I love you, Babe. I'm serious when I tell you I don't want an open marriage. I just didn't want us to end up like our best friends or worst; look at your grandparents. We don't have to do anything you don't want to do. Oh, and about that party. I had no idea what it was until Bill dragged me there. It was no biggie, just one of those novelty parties that's popping up everywhere these days. And, I didn't hook up with anyone there."

He held a straight face as he talked, but she wasn't sure she believed him. Leela had issues of her own, and there were other thoughts that kept her mind racing.

Was Samantha on to something with her new views on marriage? She and Riley had both changed over the course of their marriage. He wasn't the same man she had fallen in love with. She understood that couples could grow apart, but she didn't buy his explanation about the free Friday suggestion for a second. Maybe he was simply trying to give himself a way out. What if he'd been cheating all along like Bill, and feared getting caught?

The tub was calling her name, and she wanted nothing more than a tall glass of wine and a long phone call with Samantha about the evening's events. But she had become very cognizant of talking to Samantha while Riley was home. There were a couple of times she caught him listening to her conversation.

She never confronted him about it. She knew he'd deny it and it would lead to a major argument, but she was aware for a fact he had done it.

When it happened the first time, she didn't make much of it. But the second and third time, she told herself to limit the calls and topics she discussed with Samantha while Riley was in the house.

"See, if it was Free Fridays, you wouldn't have any problems," she muttered aloud. She had to laugh at her little joke.

As she climbed the steps, she felt her cell phone vibrate. It was at the bottom of her purse, so it would have to wait.

Immediately, she began to remove her clothes. She needed to relax and clear her head. Was Riley saying their marriage was in trouble and he thought he was sending her a lifeline?

On her side of the bed, once she dug her cell phone out, she realized the missed call was from her mother. Upon closer inspection, she noticed there were several missed calls. Instantly, Leela began to panic. She hoped nothing had happened to Big Mama or her grandfather.

With trembling fingers, she called her mother back. A shiver rippled through her as she listened to the phone ring in her ear. What was taking Linda so long to answer? Leela sighed hard.

"Hey, what's up? I see a few missed calls from you."

"Where the hell have you been?!" Linda screamed.

Leela's heart sank immediately. Panic flushed through her veins and flooded her nervous system.

"Big Mama was admitted to the hospital. I've been trying to get you for hours! Damn, Leela."

Leela felt like crap. "Oh my…where is…what happened?" She was frazzled. She couldn't focus on her ringing phone because her husband was filling her head with a bunch of bull, and here her grandmother was in the damn hospital.

"Okay, okay. I'm on my way. Where are you? What happened?"

Leela asked. She glanced around the room and tried to locate the clothes she had taken off.

"She fell. We're at Memorial Hermann, the Medical Center, not the one off I-10."

"Did you call Pah-pah?"

"What the hell would I do that for?" Linda asked. "I don't ever want to see that sick bastard until he's lying in a pine wooden box. And even then, I wouldn't break my neck to go say good-bye."

Leela sighed hard and ended the call with her mother. She quickly threw on some clothes, grabbed her purse and keys and left the bedroom. It wasn't until she strode to the front door and pulled it open that Riley's voice stopped her.

"Where's the fire?"

"My mom called. It's Big Mama; she's in the hospital. She fell," Leela stammered.

"And you was just gonna storm outta here without telling me? Leela, what the hell has gotten into you?" he asked.

Riley snatched the keys from her shaking hands. Reflex caused her to flinch as if she might react, but she stopped herself. She couldn't stop shaking.

"You're not in any condition to drive. Where are we going?" he asked.

"Memorial Hermann."

His take-control attitude and actions already made her feel better. He'd been right; she was in no condition to drive and should've told him about what had happened, but after that conversation at the restaurant, and they went their separate ways once at home, she wasn't sure how she should feel about her husband.

Inside the car, Leela turned to Riley. "Would you mind if we picked up my grandfather?"

"What kind of question is that?"

Leela quickly dialed his number and brought him up to speed. As she suspected, her grandfather was desperate to be by Big Mama's side. She didn't know how she'd get past her mother, but she felt it was the right thing to do.

When Riley pulled up outside of her grandfather's building, she confided in him that her mother would be pissed. Riley reached over and stroked her hand.

"Linda will get over it, 'cause when all is said and done, this ain't about her," he said. "Now hurry up so we can get over to the hospital. I'll deal with Linda if she starts tripping."

CHAPTER 17

Several days after Big Mama was released from the hospital something had changed in Leela's mother and Leela didn't know what to make of it. As she listened to Linda on the phone, she wondered what her mother was going through. Linda was always good at telling other people how to solve their problems, but she rarely talked about her own.

Growing up, Leela protected herself from her mother's erratic behavior by imagining herself being any place but there with Linda. Leela's older sister, Leslie, went away to college at the age of seventeen, and stayed away. Over the years, her visits slowed tremendously until they dwindled to a major holiday-only phone call.

"How far away are you?" Linda asked. "I'm less than ten minutes away."

"I'm closer. So don't make a move until I get there," Leela said.

"Okay. Well, hurry. We need to get this taken care of like yesterday."

Leela ended the call and looked over at Riley. "Thank you for helping us with this."

"You ain't gotta thank me for supporting you. We're a team, and I'm the captain of the team. That's what I'm supposed to do."

They pulled into the parking lot of Leela's grandfather's assisted-living complex and got out of the car. A few minutes later, Linda pulled up, parked, and got out of her car.

"Oh, smart move to bring Riley," she said to Leela. "How you doing, Ry?"

"Hey!"

All heads turned to Bill who jogged to catch up to the group.

"Sorry I'm late; what's up, Linda?" Bill said. He leaned over and pecked her cheek.

"Aeeey, Bill; long time no see. How are you?"

"I'm good, Linda. Good to see you. You doing okay?"

"I am now," Linda said.

Leela looked at Riley. The expression on her face was one of skepticism. She wanted to hurry up because it seemed like Linda was in a friendly mood, and that was rare.

"Listen, we don't know what to expect up there and if things get outta hand, I wanted to make sure I had enough backup," Riley explained.

Once organized, the four of them walked into the building and up to the registration desk. The building smelled like Bengay and Epsom salt. Leela wasn't sure how much she could stomach considering all that was going on.

"Hi, we're here to see the manager. I'm Linda Bishop."

Leela and Riley stood off to the side.

"Yes, our director, Mrs. Shirley Williams, has been expecting you," the receptionist said.

Leela followed behind her mother into a small office. Shirley was a hefty woman with brunette hair and blue eyes. She was friendly and greeted the group with a massive smile.

"Linda. I'm glad you guys called when you did. We didn't want to have to kick your father out, and we felt like something wasn't right, but he's such a private man, we didn't know how to help him."

"I understand, and thanks for letting us know. He doesn't know what's about to happen, but when we're done, no one else should have access to his apartment. If we move him to one of the lower levels closer to the common areas, that might help," Leela said.

"Okay, so do you guys want to call the police or do you think the building security is adequate?" Shirley asked.

"Oh. We're good. Let's go," Riley said, as he motioned in Bill's direction.

The women looked at each other, then followed behind Riley and Bill. They felt better knowing the men were there.

Outside her grandfather's door, Leela insisted they knock first.

"I don't want him to feel like we're just bursting in and making all these changes," she said. "We still have to respect his privacy."

Linda rolled her eyes, but didn't put up a fight.

Slowly, the door creaked open and Darnell peeked out. He didn't open the door completely and tried to pull it in front of his body as he stood and talked.

"Ah. What the hell you want now?!" he yelled at Leela.

Riley pushed the door open wider and they all marched in.

"Get yo' shit and get up outta here. I don't give a damn where you go, but you can't stay here anymore!" Linda yelled.

Darnell looked around as if he was considering whether he was truly outnumbered. When he eyed Bill and Riley, he seemed to retreat a bit.

Leela rushed to her grandfather's side. He eased up from the sofa and looked disoriented.

"Pah-pah, it's okay. We're here to move you to another apartment. We don't want you to stay here anymore."

When it looked like Darnell wasn't going to move, Riley stepped forward and said, "So, Bruh, where's your stuff? Is it back there? You need some help or what?"

Darnell's narrowed eyes traveled up and down Riley's frame. It wasn't hard to tell what he might have been thinking, but when Riley stepped forward, grabbed his arm and led him toward the bedroom, he didn't resist. Bill was hot on their trail.

Once the bedroom door opened, Linda balked.

"What the hell is all these people doing up in here? Y'all all livin' up in my daddy's apartment?!" she yelled.

"He my daddy, too," Darnell muttered.

"Your free ride is over. You, yo mama, yo sister, and everybody else! The gravy train has dried up! Y'all don' drained my daddy of every penny he had. Get the hell out!"

This was a nightmare. Leela knew there was no way she wanted to end up like her grandparents, or even Samantha and Bill for that matter.

As Linda carried on and made threats of arrests, Leela prayed Darnell and his entourage would do the right thing.

CHAPTER 18

"You should do it!" Samantha's eyes were wide and her entire face came alive as she sat across from Leela in the family room.

Riley was out of town on business, so Leela had invited Samantha to visit a few days. It was like the old days. They were spending time together, laughing, sharing good tea and enjoying it.

Leela wrinkled her nose. "So you're telling me I should agree to let my husband screw other women?" She sucked her teeth. "Girl, please. You divorced your own husband when you found out he was cheating." She hated when people gave the kind of advice they themselves would never take.

"Yes. I divorced his ass when I found out he'd been carrying on with his co-worker for more than a year. That's totally different. That's love or headed toward love. A man who goes out and bangs a chick because he wants something different here and there, I could deal with that," Samantha said.

Leela whipped her head in Samantha's direction. "Well, that doesn't make any sense. He can screw someone else as long as it's not the same person over and over again?"

Samantha got up and snatched her martini glass. "That's correct!" she said. "I'm going for a refill; you need one yet?"

Leela shook her head and declined the refill, but said, "I don't get your logic."

"You don't have to. I'm just telling you that if my man had come to me before he stepped out and said, let's try something to avoid divorce, regardless of whether or not I wanted to go along, I probably would've agreed. Now, you know how I feel about marriage. You know I think the whole thing is a waste of a pretty dress and lots of good liquor, and money, but if you wanna keep your man and he's asking you to give it a try, I think you should."

From the kitchen, Samantha continued, "Don't you ever get tired of screwing him?" Leela didn't respond.

"You don't have to answer that. But it's not like the man said, 'Let's move my side-piece into the room down the hall.' He said, 'One day out of the month, you can go out, have some fun and not feel guilty about it, whatever it turns out to be.' Shiiiiit! That's a win-win for you both, if you ask me!"

Samantha returned with the pitcher of grape martini and plopped down onto the sofa. "So, what's it gonna be? Are you gonna agree to Free Nights or whatever the hell it's called, or are you gonna wait for some bleeding heart chick with a tight twat and big tits to come along and give your husband a sympathy bang?"

"A what?" Leela asked as she extended her empty glass toward Samantha.

"Honey, there are women out there who actually feel sorry for married men. They feel like it's their duty to give him some sympathy pussy because the poor bastard has to wake up next to the same woman who loses her sexual desire little by little each and every day."

Leela burst out laughing. "Where do you get this foolishness? It's like ever since you got divorced, you've come up with all kinds of crazy ideas. Sympathy bang, no-spouse parties, a successful marriage has an expiration date, what the hell?"

"Laugh all you want now, but mark my word. If you don't do what Riley wants, you might find yourself sitting right next to me in more ways than one."

The following Tuesday, Leela left work early to go deal with an issue for her grandmother.

Big Mama was okay physically, but Leela was concerned about her mental state. She knew it had to be hard for her to be alone after all those years of marriage.

"Do you want to get something to eat?" she asked Big Mama as they pulled up in front of the apartment building.

"No, I'm fine. Ain't had much of an appetite," she said.

Leela was worried about that, but she knew not to bring too much attention to it.

"Okay, let me go turn this paperwork in and I'll be right back." Leela got out of the car and called her husband. "Hey, didn't you say one of your clients owns a home health care business?"

"Yeah. Why? What's up?"

She looked back at the car and saw her grandmother staring out of the windshield. Her heart sank at the thought.

"Well, I think we need someone to come in and look after Big Mama. I don't like the idea of her being alone as long as she is. It must be hard for her."

"Let me make a few calls and I'll get back to you."

Leela turned in the paperwork, then returned to the car. Her grandmother could've been a statue. She hadn't moved an inch.

"Okay, you want some pizza or something?"

"Pizza! Chile, please!"

Chuckling to herself, Leela maneuvered the car toward the back of the apartment building where her grandmother lived. She was about to really be worried if the pizza comment hadn't gotten a rise out of Big Mama.

"I could go for some smothered chicken and sweet potatoes," Big Mama said.

"That sounds great! I'll fix the sweet potatoes if you fix the chicken," Leela offered.

Her grandmother's sad eyes fixed on her. "Ain't you gotta go home and tend to your husband, Chile?"

Leela shrugged. "Riley can fend for himself for one evening, Big Mama. Besides, it's still early in the afternoon. How long does it take you to fix chicken?"

Her grandmother looked around and out of the window as if it was the first time the thought of the time of day had crossed her mind. "Umph. I guess it is still early, huh?"

"Yes, it is. So, we've got plenty of time to fix whatever you feel like eating. You know what?" Leela turned the wheel and steered the car away from the apartment. "Let's go by the store because I may want some wine with dinner this evening."

Swatting an arm and laughing, her grandmother said, "Chile, you a mess! We ain't got no business drinking no wine in the middle of the doggone day!"

"Big Mama, we both grown. If we want to get a little tipsy in the middle of the afternoon, I don't think that's anybody's business but ours!"

Four hours later, the small apartment smelled like a five-star soul food restaurant. Leela and her grandmother had made a mess. Both were feeling extremely relaxed by the time dinner was ready. They shared a bottle of wine, and over dinner, Leela decided to bring up the topic she wanted to discuss.

"Big Mama, you mind if I ask you something?"

"Ask away, Baby."

"How do you do it? You were married for more than fifty years; how do you get along without him?"

"Women are strong, Chile. You know that. Don't get me wrong; it ain't easy. But when a man shows you who he is, despite how hard it is, you gotta believe it. For many, many years, I turned my head to a whole lotta things. I never would've thought your grandfather would hurt me like that. We didn't have much, but I kept a clean house, fed him and my children and did everything a good wife is supposed to do."

Leela swallowed back tears. She wasn't trying to bring gloom over their otherwise perfect afternoon together.

"It just goes to show you. You can think you're doing it all right, and then in the end, you still wind up with shit!"

Stunned to hear her grandmother curse, Leela's eyes quickly returned to their normal size.

"I woulda though it was Sybil. Sybil Hamilton was the one woman every single wife had an eye on. I don't know what it was about that woman, but she turned some heads. She wasn't even the prettiest, but it was something about her that drove the men crazy. Now, I don't know whether Sybil did any of the things people said she did, but here I was keeping an eye on her. And while I was busy monitoring her, while she way across town, he's stepping out with my neighbor's daughter."

Leela had no words.

"I was busy focusing on a threat across town when the real enemy was right next to me and he was causing damage three doors down! Go figure."

Leela got up and rushed to the other side of the table. She took her grandmother into her arms and squeezed her tightly.

"I'm okay, Baby. I'm okay," her grandmother said.

It didn't sound like it to Leela, but she wouldn't challenge what her grandmother had said.

The wine must've been like truth serum; before long, Leela was sharing some secrets of her own.

"I just can't help but feel like he might be trying to give himself a free pass," Leela said. She had gone over the entire roll-out. She told her grandmother about the restaurant, and what happened after they had arrived home.

"But wait a minute; didn't you say you can both do what you want on this day?"

"Yeah, but what if he's only saying that because he's already doing something? I can't express it fully, but something tells me he's up to something with this."

"You've gotta go with your gut," Big Mama said.

Leela stopped and turned to her grandmother. "What are you saying?"

"I'm saying you need to go with what your gut is telling you. This ain't no decision for anybody but you to make. Your man is trying to tell you something. You just need to figure out whether you wanna listen."

Leela sighed hard.

CHAPTER 19

"Dawg, what you tryin' to do to me?" Riley asked as he walked into Bill's place and saw Natasha sitting there.

She looked just as good as ever. The sight of her made Riley hard, and he was immediately disappointed in himself. He didn't want to want her, but he did. It had very little to do with his marriage. Riley didn't like the idea of any woman having control over him; it was supposed to be the other way around.

Bill shrugged. "Sue me. I've got a soft spot for people in love."

"Wait a minute!" Natasha squealed. "Did you whiten your teeth? They look great! You look great!"

Wow! Leela hadn't even noticed and less than ten minutes with him, and Natasha picked up on it right away. He wondered how his wife had become that complacent. She hadn't even noticed the other procedure he'd had done. He didn't mind giving Natasha a pass because when she was down there, her focus was on bringing him pleasure, not aesthetics.

Bill's head snapped in Riley's direction. He squinted his eyes, then broke out into a fit of laughter. "Oh look at that. You whitening your teeth and shit now," he mocked.

Riley blew out a breath, and flipped Bill the middle finger. Riley could only imagine what his boy would say if he knew about the ball ironing.

"Nah, Dawg, real talk," Bill said as his laughter quieted and he tried to pull himself together. "It looks real good, for real," he teased. "Maybe you'll win when you enter the Miss Texas competition."

"Bill, shut up!" Natasha snapped. She turned to Riley and smiled sweetly. "I made you uncomfortable at the party. I'm sorry for that. I just couldn't resist; I needed to taste you. But I promise, I will never do anything you don't want me to, ever again," Natasha said in a sultry voice.

Riley was stunned. Had she really gone there in front of his boy? Her boldness might have stunned him, but it excited him a little, too.

Bill's eyebrows jumped up.

"It wasn't you," Riley stammered. He tossed Bill a look of death. Bill shrugged.

"It's me. I can't get caught up. Real talk, Natasha. What we had is in the past. My wife would be hurt if she ever found out," he admitted. "Why you trying to get me caught up?" Riley asked.

"Caught up how?" Natasha asked.

"Don't answer a question with a question. I'm not trying to go there. If my wife found out, I'd be dogged by headaches," he said.

"If she found out what? That I had to all but beg you to let me give you some head? Then even when I did, you act like it was nothing. Then, you ignored all of my calls and text messages. You won't even accept my friend request on Facebook."

Riley shook his head and tried to dismiss everything Natasha offered. Even when he tried to talk to Leela about Free Fridays, never once did Natasha cross his mind as a possibility. Natasha was in love. She lost out and didn't get his last name, so now she was jockeying for a position on the side. That's not what he wanted.

He wasn't on his game in her presence. He felt weak and that wasn't good for a man. He didn't plan to look backward, and he definitely wasn't trying to get caught up. That's what Natasha represented. She wanted to play house, and he couldn't afford to do that. He already had a real house and a wife in it too.

"Yo, dig this. I'ma run out for a minute. If y'all need something, hit me on the hip," Bill said. "Ima go see if I can find myself some Crest Whitening Strips or something," he muttered.

Riley used his eyes to toss Bill a disgusted glare, but Bill ignored the knowing looks and quickly scurried out of the front door.

"You can't keep doing this," he said once he and Natasha were alone.

"I know. You're right. I just wanted, needed to see you. I don't know what happened. I've held out for as long as I could. I've admired, loved you from afar, and I guess I just wanted to see what it was like, to be with you again," she admitted sheepishly.

"I get that, but we can't do this," Riley said.

"But our chemistry. When we were out on that balcony, I felt something for you. You felt the same. You wanted me; you wanted what we used to have," Natasha said.

"I love my wife."

"I know you do. But I think your heart is big enough to love more than one person at a time. And besides, I'm not asking you to leave. I want whatever you can give me. I just want to be a part of your life. I want to feel you inside of me. I want you to touch me, because since you, no other man has ever been able to make me feel the way you have. I get why you married her. I get it, but I'm not even trying to tell you to leave. I just want some time with you."

Riley shook his head.

"You deserve better. You deserve more. You should have a man of your own, Nat. You don't want this work. I know you; you'll never be satisfied for long. I can't do it."

Natasha's head hung low.

Riley gave himself a mental pep-talk. He wasn't trying to get caught up. He was willing to take extreme measures to save his marriage, not throw it away. Natasha was a bad chick. She was successful in her career. Her body was still just as tight as ever, and she looked better today than she did when she was younger. He knew he didn't need to put himself in a position where he'd be stuck in love with two women at the same time. There was no way that could end well.

"Don't answer now, please," Natasha said. She jumped up and rushed to his side.

She smelled real good. When she touched him, he flinched slightly. Riley didn't trust himself to touch her, so he stood as still as possible. He feared any sudden move might be misunderstood and he didn't want to send any mixed messages.

"Take some time to think it through. I won't see anyone else. I'll wait for you. You can have all of this. I know you want it. I know you want me," she said. Natasha took his hand and moved it to her backside. Riley didn't resist.

"I'm married," Riley said.

"Yes. I get that. But you should let me put this pussy on you. I wanna fuck you like I own you."

He wanted to crack a smile when she started using the lyrics from that song. No, he needed to stay as far away as possible from Natasha.

"I'm not available, Nat, not even part time. Listen, I'm out. Be good," Riley said and he eased out of Bill's front door.

Natasha was disappointed, but still determined.

CHAPTER 20

Before Linda even opened her mouth, Leela knew to expect something smart or sarcastic from her mother. The sour expression on her face was always a good indicator of what one could expect with Linda.

"I know this ain't what you wanna hear, but I'ma put it to you like this. I know it probably took a lot for you to share that with me, and this might hurt your feelings, but Samantha is absolutely right!"

Leela couldn't believe the words that tumbled from her mother's lips.

"I'll take it a few steps further. I say that man is trying to throw you a life line. If he came talking about let's take a break, it's because he's contemplating doing something," Linda said.

"Riley's not cheating on me. He wouldn't do that," Leela said with fleeting confidence.

Linda looked at her side-eyed as if to say, lie to yourself if you want. "Regardless of whether he is, or not, he is asking for help. Now it's up to you to decide what you're going to do."

"I don't get why I have to do anything at all."

"Chile, I wish I had the answer, but you already know, marriage is not my strong suit. What does your heart tell you to do?"

Leela contemplated that question for a bit before she answered. "Well, there's a part of me that wouldn't mind having a little freedom myself," she said. "Not to be with someone else or anything like that," Leela quickly added.

After Riley stood by her side through her grandfather's move and helped her select a home healthcare worker for Big Mama, Leela wanted to surprise him.

She'd been giving it careful thought and her mind was made up. But she wanted to break the news in a dramatic way. Her evening of romance started with a stop at Frederick's of Hollywood for some raunchy lingerie. She ordered and picked up takeout from some of his favorite restaurants and put together the perfect playlist for the evening.

Hours after everything was in place, Leela looked around at the man-cave that she had transformed into a virtual love den. Red and yellow rose petals were scattered on the floor, chairs, and tables. Candlelight flickered all over, and songs with sexually explicit lyrics were on repeat. Now, all she had to do was sit back and wait for Riley to come home so she could surprise him.

As she waited, she thought of all the ways she could share her news with him. She decided getting straight to the point wasn't the best option in this case because she still had to convince herself that this was the best thing for their future.

It didn't take long for sounds of the front door opening. The noise broke Leela's thoughts and she quickly adjusted herself on the chair.

"Leela, Babe! I'm home!" Riley yelled moments later.

She fought the urge to call out to him; she needed him to stumble onto the scene she had created. It didn't take long since she was careful to make sure every other light in the house had been turned off.

"Oh, wow!"

Leela lay stretched across one of the chairs with her legs gapped open.

Riley stepped inside and looked around like he was in an amusement park. He brought his focus back to his wife and loosened his necktie.

"Hungry?" Leela asked as seductively as she could. She waved her arm as if to show off the spread she had laid out.

Her husband's eyes grew wide. "Daaayum. You did that, Babe?!" Riley said, as he looked around his space. "Hot wings, cold beer, loaded fries, nachos? Damn!"

Leela beamed with pride.

"And, girl! You gon' get it for sure! What's that you got on over there?"

There was no point in being shy with a pair of crotchless panties, a matching garter belt, and a push-up bra with tassels that dangled from the nipples. But Leela felt a slight hint of discomfort now that she was the focus of Riley's full attention.

"Get up so I can see what you working with over there," he joked.

Leela told herself this was not the time to be shy. "You surprised, Babe?" she asked as she eased herself up from the chair.

"You damn right I am! You did good, Baby," he said.

As sexily as possible, she sashayed closer to her husband. He had already made himself at home near the display of food and drinks.

"Dance for me?" he asked, with his mouth full.

"Hoooney," Leela whined.

She never felt comfortable beneath his stare, especially when he wanted her to dance. Leela could dance enough to blend in, but she never felt she could hold her own in the spotlight.

"What? I'm your husband. You put on these sexy clothes and act like you don't want to do what's gonna come natural."

"Yeah, but dancing?"

"Aw, forget it."

Leela felt a bit slighted when he turned his full focus to the food.

"It's okay, Babe. It's just that sometimes a man wants to see his wife do something different, unexpected," he said.

Mentally, Leela coaxed herself into ignoring the disappointment in his voice. But it was Big Mama's voice telling her to follow her gut that popped into her mind.

Riley turned to her and asked, "You not hungry?"

"No, this is all for you. Go ahead, eat, because I have another surprise for you."

Riley's eyebrows rose and he stopped chewing. He looked around the room and turned back to his wife.

"You mean there's more?"

Leela nodded slowly.

Riley began to adjust his body where he sat. He rubbed his hands together and got comfortable.

"What more can a man ask for? Shiiit. Good food, good drink, and his beautiful wife decked out? I don't know how much better it could get."

"Well," Leela approached in a sexy manner. "What if I told you that I've decided we should spice things up a bit?"

Riley jerked his head in her direction. When his eyes connected with hers, Leela saw confusion in them. "Spice things up how, exactly?" Riley asked.

"I've been thinking, and I, um...I want us to give it a try," Leela stammered.

"Give what a try, Babe?" Riley asked. The excitement had all but drained from his voice.

"You know. What we talked about."

Riley's face was a blanket of confusion. He reached for some fries and stuffed them into his mouth. He shrugged and picked up his beer, took a swig, then reached for another wing.

Leela stopped him and touched his hand. When he looked up

at her, she said, "Ry. I think we should try your plan. Once a month, Free Fridays, just like you wanted."

A blank stare gazed back at her.

Leela picked up the remote and pressed a few buttons. As her husband sat in a state of disbelief, music flooded the room and she began to sway her hips.

She struggled to pay close attention to the music and the beat, but stumbled a little. It was hard for her to keep her balance on the six-inch stilettos.

When Riley's eyes focused on her, Leela tried to keep it simple. She spread her legs, gyrated her hips and shook her behind. Then she stooped down and brought her hands up the length of her body.

She had no idea what the hell she was doing, but before long, her husband moved close.

Riley played with the tassels that dangled from the front of her bra. Leela tried to focus on her strained movements. But when he palmed her bare behind and pulled her close, she lost all thoughts of rhythm.

"You look so sexy," Riley said.

By now, all Leela could do was sway her hips. He had guided her closer to his face and tugged at the bra. When he pulled it down to reveal her stiffened nipples, Leela lost all focus.

Riley used his free hand to undo his belt and unzip his jeans. He pulled her closer. With one nipple in his mouth, he guided her thigh and urged her to straddle him.

"Oh, shiiiit!"

Riley pulled her down onto his lap where his stiff erection entered her.

Leela closed her eyes and grabbed her husband's shoulders.

"Whose is this?" he moaned. He moved his hips and thrust into her. "Whose is this?"

His question was throwing her off.

Leela clung to him and tried to focus on the pleasure she wanted.

Then suddenly, Riley went limp, and just as quickly as it had started, it was over.

This could not be happening. Leela couldn't believe he had just gone limp while they were in the throes of passion. Did this mean she no longer turned him on? And if she didn't, who did?

The following Thursday evening, Riley had taken so many questions from Bill he wanted to kick himself. He should've kept his mouth shut. He was still somewhat confused by his wife's sudden change of heart. Although he didn't want to question her decision, in the back of his mind, he wondered whether she had someone on her own bucket list.

"So you had no idea whatsoever that she was still thinking about it?" Bill asked.

"Caught completely off guard," Riley said.

"Daayyum, who you banging first? I'm sure Natasha will be hyped and willing," Bill said.

Riley shook his head. "Oh, hell nah, we're not telling her a damn thing. On the real, Dawg. I still don't really believe Leela agreed to this and besides, it ain't like I'm trying to find another wife."

"Yeah, I feel you there. If we don't know anything else about Natasha, we know she wants that last name."

Thoughts of his wife and her possible desire to be with another man seemed to haunt Riley since the moment she announced her decision. Before, when Riley thought Free Fridays was the best way to save his marriage, he only wanted to give himself a break if he needed one, and of course, prove a point. But he didn't take the time to think about whether Leela would take into consideration that she would be given the same opportunity.

"Dawg! What you doin'? Daydreaming over there?" Bill snapped his fingers a few times.

Riley shook the thoughts from his head. "Oh, my bad. I'm good. I'm good. What's up?" he asked. He couldn't let Bill know that he had been having second thoughts about the whole thing. Bill would surely think it was a punk move, especially after the way Riley had gone on when they first talked about it.

"I asked when are y'all gonna start? When do y'all get a pass to bang whoever you want?" Bill chuckled. "Man, if Samantha would've agreed to an arrangement like that, who knows, we might still be together today!" Bill shrugged easily.

Something about the jokes and innuendos from Bill, made Riley that much more uneasy. He was still trying to make sense of it all.

"Ah. Next month. And, it's not really like that. We agreed to see how it goes. Then after a few months, we'll reevaluate if we have to," Riley said.

Bill winked at him. "Oh, okay. Not really like that, huh?"

Riley silently scolded himself. He needed to man up! This was what he wanted. He wanted them both to have some freedom in the marriage. It wasn't that he had a list of other women he wanted to screw, but there were things he fantasized about. There were things his wife simply wouldn't do, or if she did them, it was a big, blown-out production.

"So, what's up, Dawg? We going out or what?" Bill asked.

That's what Riley needed. Sitting around Bill's apartment talking about this free pass was only making matters worse. He needed to be out. Once he started looking at other women, he knew for sure he'd fall right in line with the idea of Free Fridays.

Besides, it wasn't like he was planning to cheat on Leela. He just didn't want them to end up like her grandparents or even their best friends.

Riley told himself that when two people loved each other and would do anything to make their marriage work, that was no cause for alarm or concern.

Hell, they were living in new and trying times; temptation was everywhere. If he slipped up here and there, that shouldn't be the end of their life together.

"Hey, Man, you okay?" Bill asked.

"Yeah, Dawg, I'm waiting on you. We leaving or what?"

"You'd think you'd be grinning from ear to ear since your wife agreed to let you get some ass on the side, but nah, ever since you been here, you've been zoning in and out acting like a lost chick," Bill joked.

"C'mon, Dawg, before I change my mind," Riley threatened.

They continued to take jabs at each other all the way to the car. But despite the distraction, Riley couldn't shake the feeling that his life was about to undergo a drastic change, and deep down, he knew he was nowhere near prepared.

CHAPTER 21

Nearly thirty days after the initial agreement, the very first last Friday of the month was less than twelve hours away. As her husband's light snores filled the air, Leela was as nervous as she could be.

She had made plans with Samantha and was actually looking forward to what the first Free Friday would hold. Hours earlier, she and Riley tried to hash out additional rules over a romantic dinner.

"So do we start Thursday at midnight, or Friday at midnight?"

"What do you think is best?" Riley responded.

Leela wanted to remind him that he had answered her question with a question, but she resisted.

"Hmm. I don't know. We both work during the day Friday, so I guess we should do something like Friday evening to Saturday evening; seems like that's what would make the most sense."

Riley simply nodded.

"But then again, what if we wanted to go away for the weekend or something like that?" she asked.

Riley frowned. He put his fork down and looked up at his wife.

"So now we're expanding to an entire weekend and we haven't even tried one Friday first?"

There was something about his tone that gave Leela pause. It dawned on her that her barrage of questions could be taken the wrong way. She didn't want her husband to think this was something she was eagerly awaiting.

"No, Riley. That's not what I meant at all. I was just trying to make sure we were both on the same page. You do realize I'm only doing this because you said it's what you wanted to do, right?"

Suddenly, it dawned on Leela that if this had been a test, she would've failed miserably. What if he never expected her to get on board with the idea? She found herself in an awkward position. Initially, she felt backed into a corner, like she didn't have a choice. But once she warmed up to the idea, and started to see the benefits, Riley was suddenly acting like she had done something wrong.

Sounds of the shower running pulled Leela from a restful sleep, even though she couldn't remember when she had finally dozed off to sleep. Moments after she pulled herself upright in bed, Riley rushed into the bedroom freshly groomed and dressed to the nines.

"Hey, Beautiful. I've got an early meeting, then hanging after work with Bill and some friends. Have a great day and I'll call you later," he said. The haphazard kiss that was meant for her forehead landed somewhere between her left eye and the bridge of her nose.

He dashed out of the master suite like it was on fire, and only traces of his cologne lingered in the air.

"What just happened?" Leela said aloud. "What time is it?"

When her eyes focused in on the clock, and the digital numbers flashed 6:45, she was baffled. Riley had never left the house so early.

Leela's work day was easy and quick. She finished up some lingering files and answered various emails. She talked to Riley around lunchtime, then right before she got off. That last conversation was the one that stuck with her. As she turned off her computer, she thought back to the call.

"Hey, Babe, are you ready?" he asked.

"Ready for what?"

"Free Fridays. Did you forget already?"

Leela didn't want to focus on the excitement in her husband's voice. Silently, she wondered whether he already had a date planned.

"I haven't forgotten. You be safe out there, okay?" Leela said.

"Damn, Babe. You act like I'm heading out to war or something. I'm about to meet with Bill and a few of the guys. What you doing? Chilling with Samantha?"

"Yeah, pretty much."

Samantha's incoming call pulled Leela back to the present.

"Hello?"

"You ready or what?" Samantha's bubbly voice asked.

"Yeah. I'm just about to leave the office," Leela said.

"Girl, bump that; we're right outside," Samantha said.

Leela's heart began to race. What did she mean "we"?

"C'mon, we ain't got all day to be waiting on you," she added.

Leela gathered her things, turned off the computer and turned off the light in her office.

"Samantha! What is wrong with you? This is my job!" Leela said through gritted teeth as she walked up on the unbelievable scene in the parking lot of her job.

Music blared, and Samantha and the man who seemed to show up wherever they were, danced as if they were in the middle of a bar room floor. Leela looked around nervously, unable to make sense of what was happening.

But suddenly, the twisted expression across Leela's face quickly melted at the sight of the gorgeous chocolate god who pulled himself up through the convertible's top.

"Hey, Sweetness! I'll bet you don't even remember me, huh?" he asked.

Leela was so shocked that the man was talking to her, she forgot all about the scene Samantha and her dance partner had created. He was handsome and his face was very familiar.

"I'm sorry. Can you turn it down a bit?" Leela asked when she finally found her voice.

Once the music was lowered, Samantha and her dance partner stopped and turned to Leela.

"Oh, I didn't even see you walk up," Samantha said. "So you ready?"

Leela's eyes bounced from Samantha to the two men with her. She knew she couldn't go off in front of them, or could she? What was Samantha thinking, bringing all of this to her job?

"Ready for what?" Leela asked.

"We're going to the Woodlands; gonna pick up some food and drinks and go relax in the room," Samantha said.

With her eyes moving from Samantha to one of the guys, she struggled to remember the last time she had discussed the Woodlands or these two men with Samantha.

Samantha eased next to Leela and whispered, "Girl, Malone has been dying to see you again."

Leela was so angry with Samantha, she didn't know whether to strangle her there or wait for the guys to leave first. "Who the hell is Malone?" Leela asked.

The DJ raised his hand without looking in their direction.

"Oh, Sweet Jesus! Girl, you must've really been fucked up that night. You don't remember when Malone had to drive your car home, and help me walk you to the door? Riley was pissed!"

Leela remembered the very first time they'd met Kent and Malone at the bar. The guys had sent a round of drinks before they came over to the table. But the second night they hung out was something else. Leela had a vague memory of that night, but she didn't remember just how gorgeous Malone was.

What she didn't forget was the Russian Morning she'd had the following day. After a night of drinking vodka, the hangover was something fierce.

Malone's skin was blue-black and seemed to glisten under the sun's rays. When he looked over at Leela and she caught a glimpse of his hazel-brown eyes, she was embarrassed.

"You look good," Malone said. "The last time I saw you, I was worried."

He was worried about her? Bits and pieces of the night flooded her mind. She vaguely remembered their time at Belvedere, the bottle service, the champagne, and too much fun. And that wasn't even the beginning of Free Fridays.

"So, okay, you guys remember each other. We need to get on the road, because I plan to be poolside in the next two hours," Samantha said.

Leela looked in Samantha's direction.

Samantha rushed to her side and whispered, "What better way to celebrate Free Fridays?" She giggled.

Leela eased into the car and once Samantha and her date climbed in, they took off toward I-45 North. She knew there was something so not right about Free Fridays. As they sat in traffic, she told herself there was no way she could carry on like that, even if it was only once a month.

She turned and saw the smile on Malone's handsome face. Maybe it wouldn't be so bad after all.

The hot sun seemed to focus its glare solely on Leela's back as she stopped at the front door. She stooped down and removed her stilettos, then eased the door open as quietly as possible. Everything about her first Free Friday had been sheer bliss, and she felt good. Samantha didn't want her to leave, but at 8:30 in the morning, Leela felt like she had overdone it and didn't want her husband to question whether she could handle Free Fridays.

As quietly as possible, she crept through the foyer and down the hall. With each step, she attempted to build the courage she knew she would need to face Riley. Once outside their master suite, Leela clutched the doorknob, took a deep breath and eased the door open.

She was stunned to realize the room was empty. Leela's feelings were crushed. Here she was nervous about the time she'd made it home and he wasn't even there. Maybe Riley was in the bathroom. Or perhaps he had fallen asleep inside his man-cave. The bathroom, closet, and every other inch of the room were empty.

Unable to control her emotions, Leela rushed to the cave in hopes of finding Riley passed out on one of the theater-style seats. He needed to be somewhere inside their house. If he'd spent the night with some woman on their very first Free Friday, Leela was ready to kill.

"So, he didn't even come home?" Leela said aloud after her eyes scanned the empty space. Her heart sank to her toes. She frowned as she dragged herself back to her empty bedroom.

As she showered, every little sound made her think her husband had finally made it home.

By the time she tied her hair up and lay down, it was close to 9:30. Nine-thirty in the damn morning after a night of guilt-free, no-questions-asked outing. Leela was beside herself. Determined not to call him, she pulled the sleep mask down and curled herself up into a fetal position on the massive bed. She couldn't remember a time when she'd felt so lonely.

CHAPTER 22

Three days after the first Free Friday, Riley still walked around his house like the floors were made of delicate eggshells. He was cautious, but he was also livid. He thought Leela would've called several times throughout the day. It may have been their first Free Friday, but what or who, had kept her so busy and occupied?

Riley's mind was all over the place. One minute he was mad that she didn't resist after they agreed to give it a try. Then the fact that she'd obviously enjoyed herself was another point of contention for him.

Was that bacon he smelled? He flicked his wrist to glance down at his watch. The date was correct; it was Monday morning, as he suspected. While his wife was often up before him, the best he expected during the week was a hot cup of coffee and toast, if he was lucky.

He walked into the kitchen, saw a place setting at the table and frowned.

"Oh. Morning," Leela sang, as she turned to glance at him quickly.

Wasn't she cheerful?

Leela hadn't offered up details about her experience, so he wasn't about to reveal anything about his own. The agreement was there were no questions and no strings. But, despite how hard Riley tried, he couldn't erase the questions he had for his wife from his mind.

They ate in complete silence. After a few moments, Leela bounced up from the table.

Riley's eyes followed her every move—closely. His mind raced with all sorts of thoughts about his wife's first Free Friday. And none of those thoughts were reassuring.

What had she done?

Was she with another man?

If she had been, was he bigger than him?

Was it Samantha's idea to hook up with another man?

Was it one of the dudes who drove them to the house?

Who was this dude and how did she know him?

How long had she been planning to get with him?

Had Bill been right all along?

"You want more eggs?"

Riley snapped out of a self-induced trance.

"Nah. No more eggs. I'm good," he said dryly.

Leela gave a half-shrug and turned back to the stove. Riley watched the way she moved and wondered whether there was an extra bounce in her step.

Had she been smiling more lately? He assumed he'd have to handle her delicately because she might harbor some anger over what he might have done. But this behavior had taken him completely by surprise. He never expected this, so he couldn't figure out how to deal with it.

"Okay, I'm about to get out of here, Honey. Have a great day," Leela said.

Riley's eyebrows rose.

He couldn't remember the last time she had fixed breakfast on a weekday morning. What was up with that? When Leela walked out of the front door, Riley released he'd been holding his breath.

"What the hell?" He smacked his forehead with his palm. He

should've said more. He should've made her tell him exactly what had gone down. Why had he become so damn emotional lately? He needed to man up!

Riley knew what he needed to do, but he had so much trouble doing it. He had warned Bill that this was not set up for Natasha to try and ease her way into Leela's place.

It seemed as if Bill just didn't want to accept that.

When his phone rang, he wanted to kick himself for thinking of his crazy friend.

"Hey, what's up?" Riley answered.

"Dude, this Friday I've got just the place for us to go!" Bill exclaimed.

"Sorry, Dawg, not gonna be able to make it," Riley said firmly.

"What? What the hell, man?" Bill said. "Don't tell me Free Fridays is already over," he asked. "Damn, we ain't even gotten the chance to get it in."

"Nah. Nothing like that. But, Dawg, it's only once a month! It ain't every damn Friday," Riley said. "And if it was, what makes you think I'd wanna spend my free time with your ass?" He blew out a frustrated breath, although Bill wasn't the true source of his frustration.

"Oh, snap! I totally forgot about that. So, what's that mean? You can't hang on Fridays anymore unless it's the last Friday of the month?"

"Nah. Nothing like that, but, Dawg, I was just away from my wife not even four days ago. I'm not gonna spend the very next weekend with your ass," he said.

"Dawg!" Bill yelled into Riley's ear. "I'm telling you, Man, you don't wanna miss this. Mark my words. If you do, you'll regret it for a very long time," Bill warned.

As he spoke, Riley's mind couldn't stop thinking he was already living with regret and he had to admit, the feeling was nothing nice.

By the end of the week, things were still strained in the Franklin household. The tension that lingered in the air wasn't because of Leela; she seemed to be adjusting well to the new arrangement. It was Riley who seemed to be having a hard time.

"So, you have to go to the hospital again?" he asked. The tone of his voice held all kinds of emotions. He couldn't shake it if he tried. "I mean, what happened this time?"

"You make it sound like I spend lots of time at the hospital," Leela said.

"Nah. It's not that. But you've gotta admit, ever since that first fall, she's been back a few times," he said.

Leela gave him a knowing glance, but didn't focus on his comment for too long.

As if an afterthought, she turned back to him and said, "Actually, once she got out after the initial fall, she had a couple of follow-up visits. Now she's back in from complications related to that same fall."

Riley shook his head. He eased a dismissive hand up as if to say she didn't need to explain, but that didn't stop Leela.

"No. Don't brush me off. I'm not sure what's been up with you lately, but if you want to come to the hospital with me, you're more than welcome to tag along. I'm sure Big Mama would be happy to see you. It's been a while."

"It ain't even like that. And I'm good. I don't know what you mean by what's been up with me, because it's all good." Riley offered what looked like a forced smile.

Leela's icy expression told him clearly that she wasn't buying what he was selling.

"So, how long are you gonna be over there?" Riley finally asked.

"As long as it takes."

Leela added a couple of items to a large bag she was packing. When she followed her husband's eyes to the bag, she stopped what she was doing, and released a deep and heavy breath. "What now?"

When she huffed, Riley wondered how the power had changed in his house. Last he checked, he was still the man and still in charge. "You got a large bag filled with all kinds of shit. I'm trying to figure out how long you plan on staying."

Leela finally laughed a little. "Oh, no, this is some stuff my mother asked me to bring for her. Don't worry, I plan to come home tonight," she said, clearly making reference to the fact that he himself had stayed out all night on their first Free Friday.

The comment caught Riley a little by surprise. He wasn't sure whether he should address it or act like he didn't notice the dig. He'd be dammed if he started answering for his actions. It wasn't even the point that she behaved as if she didn't remember the rules of Free Friday; it was that he was still the man of the house and could do what he saw fit.

"Is there something you wanna say?" he asked.

Leela frowned. She shrugged as she returned her focus back to the contents of the bag.

"Is there something you wanna tell me?"

"I keep telling you about answering my questions with a damn question! It's like you trying to hide shit!"

"Babe, you've been acting real weird lately. I'm not hiding anything, and I don't need to discuss anything. If I had something to say, I would say it, but now I'm a little confused because I don't know what it is you think I'm hiding," she said. "Besides, you're the one who's acting all strange. What's up with you?"

"I told you. I'm good," Riley insisted.

"Okay. Well, you're good, I'm good, it's all good," Leela joked.

"Cool then. Okay, well, I guess I'll go chill with Bill for a little while then. At first I told him you and I would be chilling, but I didn't know Big Mama was back in the hospital."

Nodding her head, Leela didn't add anything else to her husband's comment. Still, he watched her every move closely, and she noticed.

CHAPTER 23

"It's like she's giving up," Linda said somberly.

She and Leela stood off in a corner of the hospital room where Big Mama was being treated for yet another issue related to the fall she had sustained. It was as if the elderly woman couldn't muster up the inner strength needed for a full and complete recovery.

"I think I know what will help," Leela said. Leela was uncomfortable about the lack of progress with her grandmother's health. Big Mama's frail condition seemed to worsen weekly. After the fall, she seemed plagued by other health issues. Leela felt like the hospital staff was getting to know them all on a first-name basis.

"At this point I'm willing to try just about anything. I hate to see my mother heading down this path. I thought once we got that live-in, things would get better, but it seems to have gotten worse," Linda complained. "I wish she'd shake it off!"

"What is the doctor saying?" Leela asked. She ignored the "shake it off" comment because she wasn't in the mood to argue.

Linda looked around the room. It took a long time before she made eye contact with her daughter again.

"They're kinda confused too."

"Wait. Don't tell me they think she's faking it," Leela asked.

"No, they're saying she might need a hip replacement, but emotionally, they're not sure if she'll be able to do what's necessary to recover," Linda said. "And I agree with them. What's the point of her having any kind of surgery if she's still so frail?"

At that moment, Leela knew what she had to do. She didn't want to run the risk of telling her mother because she didn't need Linda's negativity. She told herself Big Mama's future depended on what she did next.

"I'm gonna run and grab something to eat. You hungry?" she suddenly asked Linda.

"No. I ate before you got here."

"Okay, well, I'll be back," Leela said and rushed out of the hospital room.

Leela walked down the hall and rode the elevator to the hospital lobby. She knew she'd need help if she wanted to pull off her plan before visiting hours ended.

After she made the first call to tell her grandfather to get ready, she needed someone else to help execute the plan.

When she dialed her husband's number, she remembered that he was hanging out with Bill, but figured she needed to try him anyway.

Riley answered the phone, but the music blared so loudly in the background, Leela could hardly hear her own thoughts. It frustrated her that he was out partying while she was dealing with family issues, but there was nothing she could do.

"Hey what's up? Is everything okay?"

"Yeah. I just thought you could help with a favor for Big Mama," Leela said.

"You wanted to do what?!" Riley yelled.

"I needed you to do a favor for Big Mama!" Leela raised her voice.

"Babe, speak up, I can't hear you," Riley said.

"It's okay. Hey, I'll talk to you later," Leela said.

"You sure?"

It was clear, Riley was out having a good time, so Leela ended her call with him and dialed Samantha instead. For a fleeting moment, she wondered whether he understood Free Fridays was only once a month. But she needed to focus because the clock was ticking.

"Hey, Girl, I was just thinking about you. But since you were free last Friday, I didn't know if that meant you had to be on lockdown this Friday," Samantha said. "You know I don't want to cause any trouble."

"No. I'm fine. But I'm calling because I really need a favor from you," Leela said. "Do you think you can go and pick up my grandfather and bring him to the hospital? Big Mama is back in again, and I think he might be able to help us."

"Girl, of course I can," Samantha said. "Is Riley there?"

"No. He's out with Bill. I would've asked him to do it, but they're at a party or something, so it would really help if you could pick up my grandfather and bring him here."

"Okay, let me have the information and I'll call you when we get there."

"Sam. Thank you so much."

"Leela. Don't even mention it. Now, let me go so we can hurry up. I'll be there soon."

Nearly two hours after her call to Samantha, Leela's phone vibrated and she jumped to dig it up out of her purse. Linda sat next to Big Mama's bed and talked on her own cell phone.

Leela answered the phone and moved toward the window in the room.

"Hey, Sam, what's up?"

"Girl, your grandfather is a real riot. What's the room number?" Samantha asked.

Leela told them how to get to Big Mama's room and quickly ended the call. She needed to talk to Linda before they made it up to the room. She was not prepared for the drama that was sure to unfold.

"Hey, Ma, we need to talk. Can you wrap up your call?"

Linda pulled the phone from her ear. "Don't you see me on the phone?"

"Yes. I do. And that's why I asked if you can wrap up your phone call," Leela said.

The look Linda tossed her way made Leela unsure of whether her mother would ignore her. But Leela stood her ground. She knew the clock was ticking and she didn't have a lot of time.

She stood over Linda as her mother reluctantly told the caller she had to go.

"Now, what the hell is so important?" Linda asked. She frowned as she pulled the phone from her ear.

Leela was about to answer when Big Mama stirred. The women looked in her direction. Big Mama had been drifting in and out of sleep for the past few hours.

"What you two over there hemming and hawing about?" she asked.

Seconds later, there was a soft knock on the hospital door. The door swung opened before anyone could answer. In walked Samantha, followed by Leela's grandfather.

Instantly, Linda's expression changed from hope to bitterness.

Leela looked at her. "That's what I was trying to tell you, but you wouldn't get off the phone."

If looks could kill, Leela would've been an instant corpse. Awkward glances flew around the hospital room.

But, it was the expression on Big Mama's face that said it all. Her sunken eyes brightened almost immediately. She seemed to pull herself upright even more and began to fidget with her hair.

"Hey, Ol Timer, what brings you here?" Big Mama asked. If

Leela didn't know better, she'd think her grandmother was flirting.

The only face in the room that was stoic and void of any emotion at all was Linda's. She crossed her arms at her chest and planted her feet like it would take several muscle-bound men to move her.

Leela watched as her grandparents fell into a knowing and comfortable conversation. As she and Samantha whispered to each other, Linda looked on with something similar to hatred in her eyes.

CHAPTER 24

Beneath the massive green awning at Memorial Hermann hospital's main entrance, the sounds of vehicles, chatter, and the outdoors came to a screeching halt for Leela. That's when she saw Samantha's Range Rover roll to a stop near the valet stand. The moment her eyes connected with the person in the passenger's seat, she felt her knees go weak and threaten to buckle.

"Www-hat's he doing here?" Leela asked nervously.

"Oh, Malone? Kent drove us," Samantha said innocently. "We were on our way to a vehicle auction when you called."

In that moment, unable to move, Leela felt like she had to make a split decision. Should she bolt back inside to the safety of Big Mama's room and leave later with Linda, since she didn't drive to the hospital, or take her chances and go with Samantha and the guys? She didn't need another dose of Malone. She didn't think she could handle it.

When Malone got out of the truck, then walked up and pulled her into his strong arms, Leela wanted to melt right where she stood. His mere touch sent an electric spark through her; he smelled so good, and felt better.

"Hey, Sweetness, I'm sorry to hear about your grandmother. I hope she gets better soon. Is there anything I can do to help?" he asked as their embrace ended. The sincerity in his voice made her heart nearly skip a beat.

Leela struggled to find her voice. Through her peripheral vision, she could see Samantha. When their eyes connected, Leela noticed the hint of mischief that flickered across Samantha's face.

What the hell was this woman trying to do to her?

Before she climbed into the backseat, Leela watched as Samantha and Kent exchanged googly-eyes. She rolled her own, and buckled her seatbelt the minute Malone slammed the door shut.

Leela watched as Malone darted around the front of the truck and eased in next to her. Once nestled next to her, he threw an arm over her shoulder and pulled her close. What the hell was she doing? Why didn't she run back upstairs? She wasn't strong enough for these close encounters.

"It's gonna be okay, Sweetness," he said and snuggled next to her. Leela tried to ignore the tingle that shot down her spine. She wanted desperately to send a subliminal message to Samantha asking for rescue, but it felt so good to be in his arms. She was conflicted.

Instead of signaling any kind of SOS or distress signal, she allowed herself to sink into the comfort of Malone's strong arms.

Kent took off and Leela couldn't help but wonder what they looked like. From the outside, they probably appeared like four people headed for a double-date, but for her, on the inside, a constant battle brewed.

If Riley found himself in a similar position, she'd want him to do the right thing. Samantha was a newly single woman. She could keep company with Kent and Malone, but Leela had a husband, and if her husband found out, she knew, nothing good would come from the situation.

"Hey, can you guys drop me home?" Leela finally asked. Samantha whipped around in her seat and looked back at her with confusion across her face.

"We're gonna go grab a bite and some drinks," she said to Leela.

"Yeah, it's still early. We won't keep you out too late; promise," Malone said.

Leela was so angry with Samantha, because she knew better and that Riley would have a fit if he caught a glimpse of what was going on.

"Not tonight for me, guys. I'm really tired. I think I should go home, turn in early," Leela pressed.

Kent's brown eyes fixed on her through the rearview mirror. "You know, I think Leela's got a point. She's probably not in the mood to be out on the town. How about we get some takeout, grab a movie from one of those Redboxes and chill at your place, Sam?"

"Oh, that's a great idea!" Samantha quickly added. "You're so thoughtful, Babe." She leaned over and kissed Kent's cheek.

Leela wanted to throw up a little in her mouth.

"Yeah. That's probably much better anyway," Malone chimed in. "Sweetness, your grandmother is gonna be okay," he said, and pulled Leela even closer. "I just feel it. Trust me, I'm usually right about this sort of thing."

Later, as Kent pulled up in Samantha's driveway and hopped out of the car, Leela didn't move a muscle. She waited for Malone to hop out, like she knew he would. Then she quickly reached up and yanked on Samantha's weave!

"Oouch!"

"What is your problem? You know I ain't got no business hanging out with this man!" Leela said quickly.

There wasn't enough time for Samantha's response, before both of their car doors opened.

"Ladies," Malone said, as he extended his hand to help Leela climb out of the backseat.

Leela felt like such a fraud. She watched as Samantha sashayed up the walkway and unlocked the front door.

Inside Samantha's house, the men moved around like they were daily fixtures in her space.

"Can I talk to you for a sec?" Leela asked Samantha.

"You guys go ahead. I'm gonna fix the food, and Malone is about to whip up some drinks," Kent said.

"You sure you don't need me to help?" Samantha asked as she tried to make her way toward the kitchen.

"We got it covered in here, Babe. Go talk to your girl," Kent said. He used his hands to shoo her away.

Tired of waiting for permission, Leela grabbed Samantha by the shoulder and gently shoved her toward the back bedroom.

"He says they've got it under control," Leela said.

"But I can..."

"You can come back here so I can talk some sense into you!" Leela said, as she led Samantha toward the bedroom door.

The minute they were behind closed doors, Leela pulled in a deep breath. Her eyes narrowed as she focused her stare on Samantha. "What the hell are you trying to do?" she asked.

Samantha shrugged. "I dunno what you're talking about."

"Don't play stupid with me. Why do you keep making it so easy for Malone to get to me? You know good and well that you needed to tell me you were with them!"

"Why are you trippin'? Malone knows your situation. He really likes you," Samantha said. "Girl, why you trippin'? The man knows the job is dirty. If he ain't afraid, and is still willing to sign up for the position, why not sit back and reap the benefits?"

"Sam! I am married! I can't be keeping company with some sexy man just because he likes me!" Leela screamed.

Samantha laughed.

Leela frowned.

"What's wrong with you? What's so funny?"

"You! So you admit, you think he's sexy," she said.

"Sam! I'm serious. Things are strained with Riley and me. I don't need any distractions right now."

"But Malone is so sweet. He simply adores you. Leela, when you're with him, I don't know what it is; but you're like a completely different person. He's a perfect gentleman, he's handsome, and he has a great job. What's there not to like?"

Leela stood with her arms crossed at her chest.

"Oh, I don't know. How about my husband? Samantha, I am married! You're right, Malone is all of those things and more, but I'm not trying to get caught in a lóve triangle. Besides, if he's that damn perfect, why is he still single?"

Samantha cut her eyes at Leela and a sly grin spread across her face. "See, I knew you were feeling him. You two are so cute together!" she squealed.

Leela looked at her friend like she had really lost her mind.

"Leela. We have hit the jackpot with these two. Kent is everything! He's a perfect gentleman, he's so considerate, and I think I'm falling in love," Samantha admitted.

"Well, I'm happy for you! But this is not a double-date, and I need you to respect the fact that I'm already married and I'm not trying to get a divorce!"

The smile fell from Samantha's face.

"You know what, you're right. I'm sorry. I shouldn't encourage Malone, regardless of how he feels about you. It's just that he's so sweet and the two of you are so adorable together. But I'll stop. After tonight, when he asks about you, I'll shut him down."

Leela gave Samantha a knowing look.

"I'm serious," Samantha said.

Leela was unsure of what she feared more: her lying friend or the feelings she had developed for Malone.

CHAPTER 25

Free Fridays was a recipe for disaster. There was nothing good about a married woman being able to do whatever she felt like, no questions asked, no worries about guilt. Leela looked into this man's eyes and wondered how she had lost herself so quickly.

She needed to put a stop to this before everything she knew became completely unrecognizable. After the delicious meal Kent and Malone had prepared, they were sitting around and about to watch a movie.

"Sweetness, would you like more wine?" Malone asked.

All evening long, he'd been the perfect gentleman. He was everything Samantha had described and the fact that he knew and understood her situation, but didn't seem to care, gave Leela a sense of danger and adventure.

There was the part of her that understood that if Riley ever found out, he'd break both her and Malone in two, probably with his bare hands. But Malone didn't seem like a push-over, either. Leela had a feeling he would be able to hold his own.

"No more wine for me."

Leela caught the look Samantha had tossed her way, but she didn't care. How could she get her girl to stop acting like they were two high-schoolers on a double-date? Samantha was completely comfortable despite the fact that what was going on in her house was wrong.

"Hey, Sweetness, come back here for a sec; I wanna show you something," Malone said. He stood near the hall.

All eyes followed him there even though he was only talking to Leela.

"Umph. You scared?" Samantha asked.

Leela rolled her eyes. She giggled because while they'd been curled up together on the sofa, Malone had allowed his hands to wander all over her body. It felt good. She and Riley only really touched when it was time to have sex. Their cuddle moments had vanished years ago. And Leela never realized how much she missed that kind of touching until Malone came along.

Playing along with him, Leela eased up from the couch and followed him down the hall.

The minute he pulled her into the spare bedroom, which had become something like their love nest, and closed the door, he pinned her up against it and smothered her with a wet and sloppy kiss.

Leela could barely catch her breath as he pulled back and sucked her neck.

"Malone, you've gotta stop," she purred.

Her fingers spread wildly against his bald head and seemed to pull him in closer. Everything he did to her felt amazing.

Their fingers laced together as he held one arm up and used his other hand to work her left breast out of its lace cup.

"Jesus, Malone!"

He filled his mouth and suckled her nipple like he needed whatever his lips pulled from it. Leela squirmed; she breathed hard, and tried to pull herself free.

"You're gonna make me," she whispered.

It was hot in the room. Their coupling generated the scent of sex before any penetration occurred. Leela wanted him; she wanted to let him do whatever he wanted. He felt good. Her hands traveled along his muscular back and again, she pulled him closer.

"Wait, let's move to the bed," she said.

Leela couldn't believe she had made the suggestion, but she had.

When Malone released the hold he had on her, their eyes connected.

"You sure about this, Sweetness?"

That question brought Leela to her senses. She shook her head. "No, I'm not. I'm so sorry. I got caught up in the heat of the moment."

"No, I'm sorry. It was my fault. I couldn't resist. Here, let's go back out there and watch the movie. I'll be on my best behavior. I promise."

"Okay. I think that's a great idea. But I need a moment." Leela motioned toward his crotch. "It looks like you do, too."

Malone looked down. "See what you do to me?"

"What do you mean you looking for Leela?" Riley asked into the phone. He had gone from zero to sixty in less than a minute, and he was pissed. This was more than embarrassing. What did it look like, his mother-in-law calling the house to find his wife?

Where the hell was she if she wasn't with her grandmother like she was supposed to be? From what he knew, they were all supposed to be at the hospital. That was what Leela had told him she was doing after work. Now Linda, who was at the hospital, was calling and looking for her?

"Well, let me figure out where she is and get back with you," he said, as calmly as he could. It was all he could do to hold his composure as they talked. The last thing he needed was Linda's nosey ass all up in his business.

"I called Samantha, but she ain't answering, either, so I figured she'd be home with you by now."

"Yeah. I got that, Linda. Look, lemme holler at you in a few. I'll tell her to call."

"Okay, but is everything okay over there, Riley?"

That's exactly what Riley was afraid of. He knew how people thought. His wife was out late at night, not answering her phone, and of course it looked like the man had lost control. Oh, not on his watch! He'd get to the bottom of this crap and put Leela back into her place where she belonged.

"Yeah. It's all good. I'll have her call you," Riley said.

But his nosey mother-in-law just wouldn't shut up! She kept yapping and yapping and all he wanted to do was get her off the phone so he could find his wife.

"Linda. I said I'll have her call you."

That firm voice finally did the trick. Riley was so pissed he could draw blood. What the hell was Leela thinking?

Minutes after he finally wrangled Linda off the phone, he called his wife's cell. She answered by the fourth ring, far too long for his taste.

"Hello?"

Riley didn't respond right away. He tried to listen to hear whether sounds from the background would give an indicator of where she was and what she was doing.

"Hello?" She sounded frustrated.

"Where the hell you at?" Riley asked.

"Uh. What's wrong?"

"Damn, Leela. How many times do I have to tell you about answering my questions with another friggin' question? Where are you?"

"I'm just trying to figure out why you're so pissed off, that's all.

I tried calling you earlier and you didn't answer. I needed you to pick up my grandfather and bring him to the hospital."

"Don't even try to act like you're at the hospital because I know you're not there! Leela, I'm not for this bullshit!"

"Riley, cut it out!"

"Who you talking to like that?"

Leela lowered her voice. "I'm sorry. I'm on my way home now," she stammered.

"That's beside the point. I asked where you are now. I didn't ask whether you were on your way home."

Leela sighed.

"This shit has got to stop! I'm not tolerating this kind of behavior. It's damn-near one-o-clock in the damn morning and I'm calling all around the city looking for my wife? Got your mama questioning me when you're supposed to be at the hospital with her? Shiiiit. You got me messed up!"

"Riley, I said I'm on my way," Leela repeated.

"You bet your ass you are!"

Leela didn't have to tell him where she was, because he already knew. Once she hung up the phone, he dug up his iPad and logged on to the app to confirm his suspicion. Yeah. Things needed to change in the Franklin household and that change needed to happen like yesterday.

CHAPTER 26

Thoughts of Malone stayed on Leela's mind way more than she wanted. Oftentimes, she caught herself comparing Riley to him, and she knew that wasn't fair. But it was so hard for her to stop.

Riley was so rigid at times. Malone was carefree, like a dreamer. While Riley helped out with anything physically related to her grandparents' breakup, Malone was there emotionally. He seemed to get it. He understood the craziness of a divorce after such a long marriage.

On date night with her husband, Leela sat inside the darkened theater and zoned out on the previews for upcoming movies. Her mind started to drift to thoughts of a perfect world. Malone was an all-around sweetie, but Riley exuded strength and took control when she needed it. Was there a way she could have them both?

"Oh, Jesus! I want him," she muttered aloud.

She quickly glanced around to see if anyone had heard her confession. The theater was full, but the loud Dolby sound system had drowned out her voice. Her declaration was still safe. It was the first time she had verbalized it, but not the first time the thought had crossed her mind. When she noticed no one had paid any attention to her, Leela eased into the bucket seat.

She felt pathetic. On date night, she couldn't stop thinking about her sidepiece. Leela jumped, startled, when her cell phone vibrated after a text message came through.

When she saw the name "Mary" pop up on the screen, she smiled. It was a message from Malone and it was sweet and short.

I MISS YOU!

Leela looked around. She didn't dare respond to Malone's text message. She was just glad her husband still hadn't returned from the concession area.

There was no denying that she was now officially doing wrong. She thought about how put-out she was when Riley first presented the idea of Free Fridays. Now, she felt herself counting down the weeks and days until the next month.

It didn't help that Samantha seemed to do everything she could to help Malone. Leela thought about the conversation she'd had with Samantha just before she'd left Samantha's place.

"I can't be here. I can't be alone like this with him. I can't do this," Leela said in a panicky voice. Her adrenaline raced as she moved around the room, scared but excited. She needed to get her stuff together and get home before her husband sent out an official search party.

Samantha giggled like they were schoolgirls enjoying the sweetest joke.

"Listen, I wasn't supposed to say anything, but the guys are trying to plan a trip for us next month," Samantha said once her giggles subsided. She threw up her arms in mock defense. "Hold up; hold up before you start going all ballistic; we're planning it around the next Free Friday. That way you won't be acting all holy and stuff," she said.

Leela froze. Her eyes grew to the size of saucers. Her mouth slowly fell open, until it nearly hit the floor. She couldn't believe her ears.

"Before you go all ham on me, it wasn't my idea," Samantha defended.

"Have you heard anything I've said? Are you even listening to me?" Leela asked.

Samantha shrugged. "What?"

"Sam! I am married! I can't just run off with you, Malone and Kent! We are not kids on a double-date!"

"Girl, please! Why are you tripping? I said we're planning it around your next Free Friday." Samantha shrugged again. "Can you imagine what Riley is doing during his free time? And if he's with Bill, Girl, please!"

For a moment, Leela stood and watched her friend. She didn't understand why Samantha behaved like they were back in their college days. Although they didn't know each other then, that was the last time that Leela had thrown caution to the wind and behaved as irrationally as Samantha was suggesting.

Samantha danced around the room. "Girl, Malone is totally feeling you. All he does is talk about you. I'm just glad you guys found each other, because he is so sweet!"

Leela looked on as Samantha talked about the trip and how much fun they were going to have.

Suddenly, Samantha stopped and looked at Leela. She twisted her face and said, "Somebody, please, call the Pope, because apparently, we have a saint!" She said it in the most dramatic way, before she opened the door and walked out.

"Babe!"

"Babe!" Riley's loud whisper interrupted Leela's thoughts. She jumped up and helped him by grabbing some of the snacks he struggled to balance in his hands.

"Sorry," Leela said.

"What were you doing? Daydreaming?" he asked, as he settled into the seat next to her.

"Shhhhh," said Leela as she stuffed her mouth with popcorn.

She knew for a fact that her husband didn't want to know what she had been daydreaming about. Even as the movie started, she thought about how pissed her husband had been with her lately.

"I don't want you hanging out with her! It's just that simple," Riley had said.

Leela wasn't ready for a fight. She needed a shower so she could wash Malone off of her skin. While the soap would help with that, she couldn't think of anything that would get him out of her system.

Once things settled down with Riley over the amount of time she'd been spending with Samantha, they agreed they needed some time together.

That was where the movie came in. But for the life of her, Leela couldn't keep her mind on the movie, Riley, or their marriage.

Days later, Riley was still puzzled by the sudden deterioration of his home life. He grabbed the cell phone and answered before it rang for a second time.

"I just want to see you," the whining voice said.

Riley rolled his eyes as he listened to Natasha begging on his cell phone. He felt anxious, but the anxiety had nothing to do with Natasha. He hadn't changed his position on her. It didn't matter how many times he told her there could be nothing more between them, Natasha wouldn't let up. A part of him admired her persistence, although he'd never tell her that. Riley knew any compliment or positive comment would be like a green light, telling her it was okay to keep up the pursuit.

"Hey look, I can't talk to you about this right now," he said, with one eye on the door. His voice was low as he approached the master bedroom.

"Why not? I really need to see you. Can you get away for about an hour?" she asked.

The desperation in her voice made Riley curious, but he had bigger issues than Natasha. His mind was fixed on whether he had made a major mistake with his wife.

"No, I can't. Hey, listen, I'ma have to holler back at you at another time."

"But, Riley," he heard her voice say as he moved to end the call.

What was going on over at Samantha's? Why did Leela need to spend so much time over there? Could Bill have been right all along? Was he too blind to see what was happening literally underneath his nose?

Riley shook the thoughts from his head. He was second-guessing himself at every turn and it was driving him crazy. He stepped into the bedroom and heard the shower running.

Quietly, he moved across the room and picked up Leela's cell phone. Instinct told him to put it down. But he reminded himself that as the man of the house, everything in it technically belonged to him. It wasn't an invasion of her privacy. And just as he was about to lay it back down, it vibrated. A text message came through; it was from Mary.

I hope everything is good with your grandmother.

Riley put the phone down. Mary must've been a co-worker or something, although he couldn't be sure. This mess was driving him crazy. Free Fridays was supposed to save the marriage, not turn him into a crazy detective who snooped around on his wife out of fear she was cheating.

Riley was doing something he'd never thought was possible and it chilled him to his core.

He was losing control.

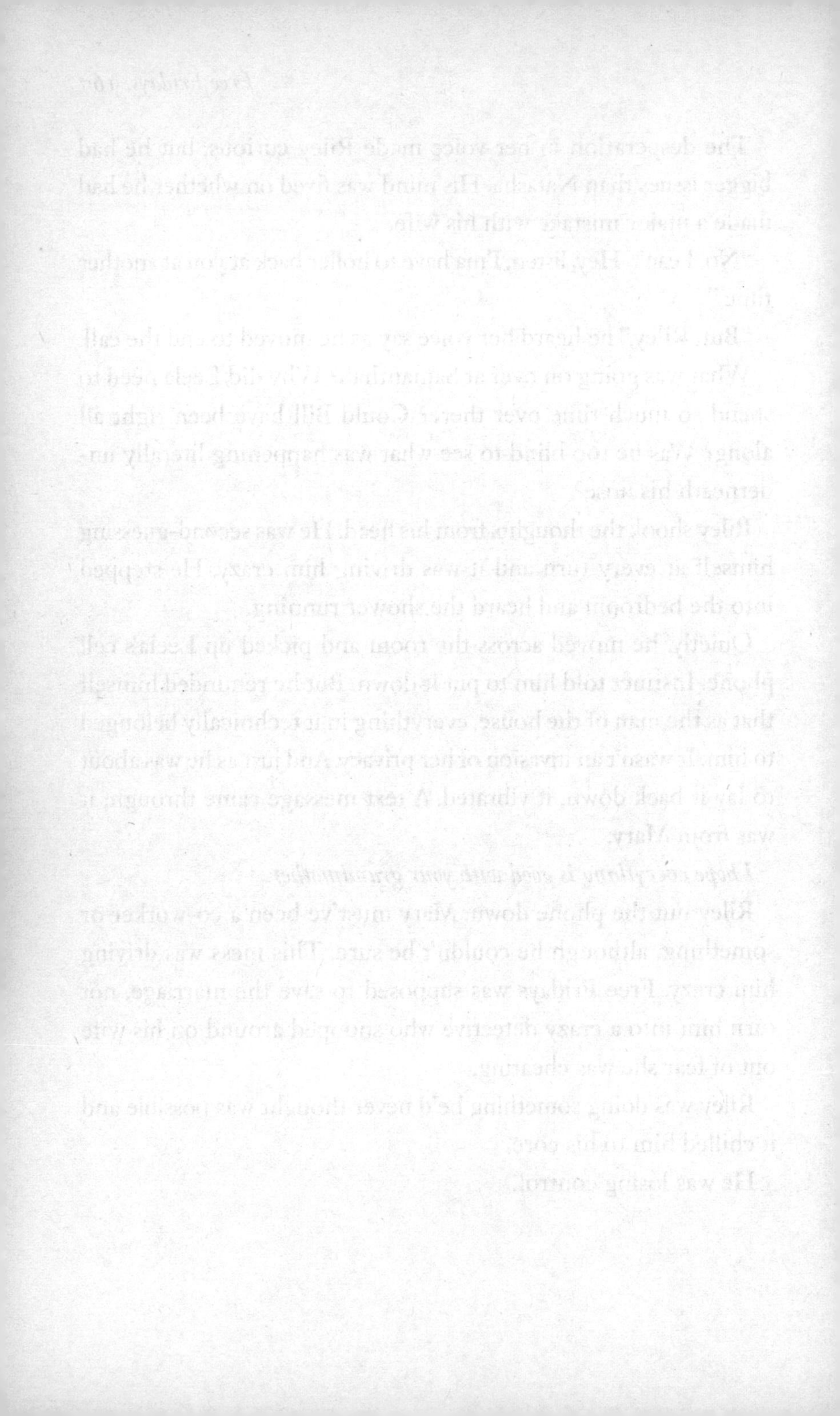

CHAPTER 27

Leela strolled through the busy, crowded restaurant. Aromas from seafood dishes, fried appetizers, and fruity cocktails mixed in the air and tingled her senses, as she made her way toward the table near a large window. She was meeting her mother and grandmother for a late lunch, and while her stomach growled a bit with every step she took, there was another emotion that was more overpowering.

It was the Thursday before the next Free Friday and Leela couldn't calm her excitement.

"Big Mama, you look so good; I'm glad to see you're feeling better," Leela said as she approached the table.

Her grandmother stood, and the two hugged and kissed. The minute her grandmother took her seat, Linda chimed in. "Umph. Ask her why she's suddenly glowing all over the place," she snarled.

"Cut it out," Big Mama said to Linda and swatted at her arm playfully.

Leela looked between the two, a bit uneasy; she wasn't sure what she should say.

"I don't care why you look great. I'm just glad you're out of the hospital and you're starting to look like the Big Mama I've known all my life," Leela said with genuine excitement, as she pulled out a chair and took a seat.

"This is all your fault, you know," Linda added.

Leela whipped her head in her mother's direction and frowned.

"My fault? What did I do?" The confusion on her face was hard to ignore.

"You brought that loser to the hospital and ever since, those two have been two peas joined at the hip," Linda said. She motioned toward Big Mama.

Before Leela could respond, Big Mama spoke up.

"Linda, I don't expect you to ever forget what your father did. It was wrong. It ended our marriage, and I will never forget, but you must forgive him. If you can't do it for me, Honey, do it for yourself. You've got to free yourself of the extra baggage and the energy you devote to it."

"I can't. I will always hate him. I can't even stomach the fact that you can look at him even though you know that he's a lowdown cheating dog," she said.

Big Mama reached over and touched Linda's hand. "But, Sweetie, that's what I'm trying to tell you. No one is saying you should forget what happened; I don't think any of us can. But if you carry around all of that hate, it's going to destroy you. He didn't do that to you; he never broke the vow of being your father. He provided for you, was there emotionally and you never went to sleep hungry or in fear; he's still your father."

"I guess you agree with her, huh?" Linda said, as she motioned toward Leela.

Leela shrugged. "I kinda do. I'm still mad and hurt over it all. But that's their issue, not ours. Besides, I'm glad we got Pah-pah away from those leeches. I know what he did was wrong, but I guess I kinda felt like that's between him and Big Mama, and if she's able to move past it, I think we should too."

Despite what she said, Leela felt like such a huge fraud. How could anyone turn to her for moral advice? There were days she literally feared being struck down by lightning.

"Oh! I forgot. Why would I expect someone who's taking part

in some open marriage mess to agree that when you take a vow, it should mean you don't carry on a secret life with another lover," Linda said sarcastically.

Leela sat dumbfounded. Warm embarrassment quickly washed over her as she searched for the words to throw back at her mother.

When Big Mama's eyebrows knitted in confusion, Leela wanted to reach across the table and smack her own mother. But she knew better. Instead, she sat and quietly wished she could vanish right where she sat.

Leela simply went through the motions over lunch. Her mind was filled with comments her mother had made when she'd first turned to her for advice about Free Fridays. Now, after she had all but suggested her daughter use an open mind approach, she ridiculed her choice? Leela fumed as she sat there. Thank God she had already confessed it all to her grandmother.

Leela was pissed at Linda, but she was determined not to ruin lunch. For the first time in a very long while, that part of her life was beginning to look like she remembered it. Now if only she could find the happy medium and pull her home life into something similar, she might be able to make it.

A worrying thought entered Leela's head as the liquid burned what felt like a fiery trail down her throat. She was fucked up! There was no other way to put it. All that was missing was the blurry vision and the slurred speech.

"No more for me!" Leela managed the minute her voice came back. But her eyes were still watering as she tried to fight off the effects of the alcohol.

"Fucky, fuck!" Samantha stammered. "You are such a lightweight! What's that, three rounds?"

Leela sighed and turned her blurry eyes to her friend and partner in crime. "Uh, excuse you! That's three rounds of shots on top of three top-shelf margaritas!"

"What's taking them so long?" she asked.

Samantha shrugged and drained her glass.

"But we're just getting started. It's Free Friday! It's Free Friday," Samantha sang and wiggled in her seat. The way her arms flared in the air and the number of eyes that took notice told Leela she should brace herself for an interesting evening.

"Hey, their next round is on me," a man said, as he slid close to the bar and stood in the space behind Samantha.

He was tall and husky. He wasn't fat, but it looked like he'd allowed his once muscular body to slip away.

"Oh, I'm good. No more for me," Leela quickly volunteered, then hiccupped.

"What about you, Thickness? Lemme buy you a drink, since Slim over there can't hang," he said.

"Oh nah, Playboy, we got this," another voice said.

Leela looked up to see Malone and Kent approach. Malone walked up and kissed Leela full on the mouth. He even slipped her a little tongue, which she accepted, as if it was the most natural thing to do.

The other man looked back and forth between Samantha and Kent as if he didn't understand. But when Samantha turned her full attention to Kent, the man eased away from the spot behind her and made his way to the other end of the bar.

"Can't leave the two of you alone for a few minutes, huh?" Kent said, as he summoned the bartender.

"What can I get for you?" the bartender asked.

Kent looked around, then said, "Give me Herradura Tequila with lemon juice on the rocks." He looked over at Leela and Malone. "What y'all drinking over there, Bruh?"

Malone turned and said, "I'll take a beer, but my girl says she needs water."

"Water? What? It's still early. She going on water already?" Kent asked.

"Lightweight," Samantha added. "Baby, I wanna try your drink."

As they talked, Malone's words swam around in her head.

"My girl says she needs water!"

When did she become *his* girl? She was very married, but when he kissed her on the mouth, Leela didn't resist. Suddenly, she eased closer to him and snuggled up as if doing so was another natural thing to do.

Everything happened so quickly. From the hotel lobby bar to the room with a view, Leela's head was spinning. She wasn't sure whether it was the alcohol or the sheer adrenaline pumping through her veins.

Behind closed doors, Malone wore a sly grin, and his eyes were ablaze with lust as he hovered over Leela. When his mouth covered hers, she shivered with excitement and raw intensity. By the time she came up for air, she painstakingly groaned his name.

"Shit. You are so sexy," said Malone.

Sheer electricity passed through Leela like she'd been struck by lightning. A tingle shot down her spine and that was after only one long, scrumptious kiss.

Leela was in trouble.

CHAPTER 28

All of the thrill had vanished from Free Fridays for Riley. He hadn't even been able to really enjoy the benefits of being able to do whatever he wanted because he remained in a state of constant worry.

What was Leela doing and how was she suddenly such a fan of the day he all but begged her to be a part of?

Riley was seconds away from confronting his wife. But he told himself that would only make matters worse. It would prove Bill's point, and it would make his wife suspicious, since the whole damn thing was his idea in the first place. Besides, he knew she was going to Samantha's. But that knowledge didn't stop his mind from racing with thoughts about what all the two of them would be doing.

"You okay, Dawg?" Bill asked, as he brought a couple of beer bottles to the table.

"Yeah, I'm straight."

"You sure don't sound like it." Bill eased one of the bottles in front of Riley.

There was nothing interesting about being at Bill's on Free Fridays. Riley wondered whether his friend got some pleasure out of his misery. Hell, he didn't care.

"What are we doing tonight? Let's go by Sam's," Riley suggested.

Bill frowned. "You serious, Man?"

"Yeah. I wanna see what's going on over there. It's one thing to look on an iPad and see what's what, but I wanna swing by; you know, pop up," he said.

Bill nodded. He took another swig of his beer. But suddenly he leaned in closer and looked at Riley.

Riley thought it would be his wife who would throw in the towel first, but he found himself very close. Nothing had gone the way he'd expected, and the more he thought about it, the less he wanted to know just what was really going on at Samantha's house.

"Okay, after we finish these," Bill said a second later. He raised the half-empty beer bottle. "Now do you get what I'm saying about marriage?"

"Man, that don't prove nothing. Yeah, you and Sam didn't work out, but I don't necessarily agree that given the opportunity, any woman would cheat. Hell, we don't even know for sure that that's what's going on with Leela. For all we know, the two of them are going out to party up like the good ol' days," Riley said.

Bill sipped more beer and nodded. He didn't say anything to counter Riley's suggestion.

"Don't give me that poor ol' bastard look," Riley said.

Bill frowned and moved the bottle from his lips. "You still wanna go over there?"

"Nah, Dawg. I'm good. I'm about to get another brew. You want one?" Riley asked, as he rose.

As Riley walked into Bill's kitchen, there was a knock at the front door.

"I'll get it," Riley said. He pulled the front door open and found a pizza delivery guy there.

"Two large meat-lovers with wings and breadsticks," he said.

Riley looked over his shoulder. "Why didn't you say you ordered pizza, Man?"

"Shit! I forgot. Thought you might want something to eat on while we figured out what to get into tonight."

"Good looking out," Riley said. He reached for his wallet and paid for the food.

Over pizza, wings, and beer, they talked more about their options for the night.

The next time a knock sounded at the door, Riley looked at Bill.

"Come in!" Bill yelled, instead of going to the door.

Riley frowned.

"What? We eating, Man!" Bill frowned.

Natasha opened the door and strutted in. "Hey, guys. Hope I'm not interrupting anything."

Suddenly, Riley felt like he might have lost his appetite.

"I knew you'd be over here, and I wanted to talk to you face-to-face. You said you were gonna call me back last week, and I never heard back from you," she said, as she walked all the way into the living room.

Natasha turned to Bill and said, "I knew you wouldn't mind. But I really need some alone time with him."

Bill got up and grabbed one of the pizza boxes. He opened it, tossed a few wings and some breadsticks inside, then walked out of the room.

"Holler if you need me, Bruh," Bill said over his shoulder.

Riley wanted to tell him to take Natasha too. But she wouldn't budge. The minute the door closed, she repositioned herself and eased between Riley's legs.

"I can't do this," he murmured.

"Let me suck your dick," Natasha begged. "I miss you; I miss the way you taste. I know that wife of yours won't give you the kind of head I know you like."

"Natasha, right now, my mind is all over the place. I can't," Riley said.

"It's Friday," she countered. "I know what that means for you. A good blow job from me won't even count. Let me help you feel good. Let me take some stress off your mind, Baby," she purred.

Before Riley could refuse again, Natasha reached for his crotch and grabbed a handful. She squeezed and stroked him.

"Natasha, seriously," Riley said. But his voice sounded shallow. He wondered whether she could sense his weakness.

"Come, Daddy, let me do this for you," she purred.

Riley flinched, and Natasha dropped to her knees and moved in for the kill.

The last thought that ran through his mind, before his eyes rolled to the back of his head was that Bill had gone and told her about Free Fridays! Gone from his head was the thought of driving past Sam's house.

Samantha sat at a table near one of the windows. She glanced down at her watch a few times and started to get a bit antsy. Why did she agree to this in the first place? There were at least one million other things she'd rather be doing.

She picked up her phone and checked it again. She was going to wait for another ten minutes; then she'd leave. What did she look like sitting and waiting on a man who all but despised her? She didn't know what he wanted with her anyway.

"Hey, thanks for waiting. Sorry I'm late."

At first, Samantha didn't respond. She hated to be kept waiting and always thought it was rude when people were late. It was even worse when she was forced to wait on someone she didn't want to meet with in the first place. She eyed him suspiciously. "So, what's going on?" Samantha asked. There was no need for fake pleasantries.

They were at the 59 Diner in Stafford, and she didn't have lots of time. Even if she had all the time in the world, he was the very last person she wanted to spend time with.

"Why did you want to meet with me?" Samantha asked before he could settle into the seat across from her. She didn't even attempt to mask the sarcastic tone in her voice. She wasn't happy about being there and didn't care whether he knew it.

"I'll get straight to the point," he said. "I think you're a bad influence on Leela, and I think you need to back off."

Samantha looked at him side-eyed. She couldn't believe her ears.

"Uh. Leela is a grown woman. You act like we're in grade school or something. I can't force your wife to do anything she doesn't want to do," she said.

With an adamant shake of his head, Riley's narrowed eyes zeroed in on Samantha.

But she remained cool under his glare. He may have walked around thinking that his biceps and muscles made others fear him, but she wasn't the least bit afraid.

"If I knew this was the kind of bull you asked me to come here for, I would've hung up the second you called," she snarled.

"So that's how you wanna play this then?" Riley leaned back in his seat. He blew out an exhausted breath.

Samantha frowned. Her eyebrows inched upward. "What the hell are you talking about? If you think your wife has done or is doing something, maybe you should be talking to her instead of me!"

Defiant, Samantha arched her shoulders and folded her arms across her chest. She had made her position crystal clear. He could accept it or not, she didn't care.

"Look, I ain't got nothing against you. I get it. I get you are single now, running around proving you still got it and all that shit, but what I'm saying is, you don't need to drag your friend down with you," Riley said. He used a finger to jab his words and point across.

Samantha jumped up from her seat. "Drag her down?" she huffed. "You have lost your damn mind. Look. What's going on or not going on with you and Leela ain't got nothing to do with me!" She tossed him one final look, then suddenly turned back. "I've told you before, ain't nothing about me headed in a downward direction. I never liked your ass in the first damn place! Go beat on your chest and try to bully someone else! I'm done!"

Before Riley could say another word, Samantha stormed out of the restaurant and never looked back.

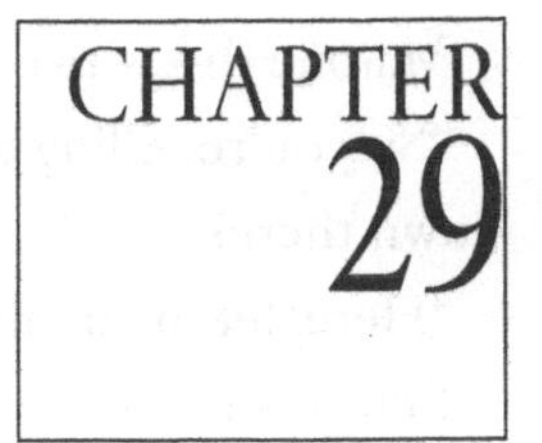

CHAPTER 29

Leela might have been fully satisfied, physically, but emotionally, she was a train wreck. She couldn't bear to look at her own reflection in the mirror for too long without the strong urge to upchuck. Despite how hard she tried, she couldn't wrap her mind around how she had landed herself right in the middle of a scandalous love triangle.

Because the bulk of her time spent with Malone was during Free Fridays, technically, she didn't have to confess anything to Riley about what she had done, but she found the weight of that secret was like dragging a large cement block around.

Besides, who spent mornings sipping champagne and eating strawberries?

"Wanna know a secret about one of the many benefits of strawberries for women?" Malone had asked.

His deep voice was so sexy to her.

"I didn't realize there were many benefits," Leela had said as she took a bite of one.

"Come over here so I can whisper it in your ear," Malone had said, wearing a sly grin.

Leela had leaned in close.

She'd giggled after he whispered in her ear.

"I'm serious."

"You're full of it," Leela said, as she pulled back and laughed at his comment.

Malone threw two fingers up. "Scout's honor. I'm serious."

"So you're telling me that eating strawberries makes it sweeter down there?"

"Here, let me double-check and I'll tell you," he joked.

Before she could stop him, he had eased his way between her thighs again. Blissful pleasure was right around the corner and she enjoyed every bit of it.

The situation with Malone had gotten completely out of control.

There was no way she was about to give in to more thoughts about him. She would throw herself into her marriage; she had a good solid three weeks before the next Free Friday rolled around. She could get that man out of her system and do what a good wife was supposed to do. Couldn't she?

She rose from her mid-afternoon nap and had a sudden urge to go and find her husband. That was part of the problem. They didn't spend enough time together. She and Riley moved around their large house like roommates at times. He spent a great deal of time in his space, and she was confined to her own. Before Free Fridays, it didn't bother her as much.

Leela was tired of it. She was about to try and shake things up a bit. She decided that if she brought some spontaneity to their marriage, she'd remember what she had in her husband and would be better able to resist Malone. Forget the fact that he had completely ravished her in her dreams, or the fact that he sent sweet text messages regularly to let her know she was on his mind; she could resist all of that.

Leela strode through their home and glanced lovingly at the black and silver picture frames that captured images of their once happy life together. She was confident they could reclaim that and then some; all she had to do was focus on what was important.

"I thought we could go see a movie or go out to dinner," she said as she stood in the doorway of Riley's oasis.

She'd been standing there for a while before she let her presence be known. She watched her husband and wondered how she had fallen so quickly for another man. Riley had his issues, but who didn't? When did she fall out of love and into lust and when did that lust morph into so much more? The truth was, she had fallen for Malone as if it was one of the most natural things to do. And for Leela, that was scary.

"Yeah, a dinner and a movie, that'll work," Riley said as he turned to look at her. "Give me a few minutes."

Leela turned and walked away. Of course she could do it; she had to. Her marriage depended on it.

A week before the next Free Friday, Riley sat on a table at the spa. He had yet to receive a compliment about it, but he knew the procedure had made a difference. He felt better about himself and that was all that mattered. His thoughts were broken when a man in a white lab coat walked back into the room.

"Do you have any more questions?" he asked.

"No. I think we're good. Oh, wait, how long will this take?"

The man picked up the clipboard from the nearby counter and flipped through a couple of pages.

"Well, the typical Male Laser Lift usually takes about forty-five minutes," he said.

Riley shook his head. "Yeah, I know that. I meant, before I start seeing the results I want."

"Oh. I'm sorry. Yeah, this is your third treatment, right? You should've seen results after the first time. We're talking lasers here, so discoloration, hair, and some of the wrinkles are zapped away immediately." The technician flipped through more pages. "Why, are you not seeing any results at all?"

A hint of alarm eased into Riley's green eyes.

Thoughts of what Bill would say if he knew that Riley had resorted to 'ball ironing' flashed through his mind once again. The truth was, lately he felt himself trying to correct quite a few things that never seemed to bother him in the past. How could he compete with another man when he had no idea who dude was? There was no other man! He was the man! He was the one and only man! If Leela dared step out on him, she'd realize that no other man would ever take his place. Look at Natasha. After all these years, she'd come to realize what he already knew: real men are hard to find.

"No. It's good. I am. I was just wondering how many more times I need to have the procedure done; that's all."

"Oh. Okay. Well, it's really up to you. When you're satisfied, we can stop."

Riley didn't respond.

"Are you ready?"

"Yeah, I'm good."

He eased back onto the table and spread his legs.

Later, as he was leaving the spa, Bill called. "Yo, Dawg, where you at?"

Nervously, Riley looked around. Had he jinxed himself with thoughts of Bill during his secret procedure?

"Why? What's up?"

"Now I need a reason to check in on my boy?"

"Nah, nothing like that," Riley said. "Actually, I'm just leaving an appointment; about to head back to the office."

"Oh shit, what you getting done now? Wait, lemme guess, more teeth whitening? Oh, no, maybe it's one of those Brazilian wax jobs! Damn, Playboy, you got it bad. You add all this extra grooming, with the monthly cycle, and all your new feelings, and I might need to go file a missing person's report," Bill chided.

"Man, chill, all that ain't even necessary."

"Oh, well, tell me something. I'm just checking, 'cause my real boy is straight M-I-A."

"I was meeting with a client. You know, the kind of work you used to do?" Riley said.

"Oh. Okay. I see you got jokes. But that's all right. I'm almost back. My lawyer has a meeting in a couple of weeks. Looks like I should be back at the ol' salt mine by the end of the month if all goes well."

"That's what's up, Dawg! That's what's up."

Riley pushed Bill's jokes to the back of his mind but only temporarily. As they went back and forth, he steered his car into traffic and thought about whether he was losing his confidence.

He already felt like his wife had checked out. The last thing he wanted to do was start getting all emotional like Bill had accused him of being.

As they wrapped up their call, Riley made a decision. It was time for him to step up and do what men are supposed to do, and he meant that in all aspects of his life: at the office, at home with his wife and even with Natasha.

CHAPTER 30

A few days later, as she strolled through the office and toward her assistant's cubicle, Leela felt like something strange was going on. At work, she prided herself on her ability to remain beneath the surface. She was friendly to everyone, but her guard remained up at all times. And since she wasn't one to socialize much at work, she ignored it when she saw some of her colleagues near the water cooler and others who whispered as she passed.

That was what cheating did; it made you paranoid. For all she knew, her co-workers probably weren't even focused on her.

Leela's cell phone rang before she arrived at her office door. It was Linda, so she took the call.

"Hey, Mom," she said.

"So?"

"So what?" Leela knew why Linda was calling. Leela had just returned from lunch with Big Mama and her grandfather. They weren't reconciled, but saw each other weekly and Leela was convinced it was doing wonders for her grandmother's health.

"What did he have to say for himself?" Linda asked. Her voice held its usual sour tone.

Leela passed her assistant who mouthed something and pointed toward her office door.

"I don't understand," Leela said.

"I'm still not sure that she should be keeping company with him. I can't get over what he did to my mother—hell, to us all," Linda whined.

"Well..." Leela sighed. "I get that, but while you're over there holding him accountable or whatever it is that you're doing, it looks like they're moving on with their lives."

"Oh, God! Are you trying to get them back together?" Linda asked.

Leela clutched the doorknob and opened the door.

"OhMyGod!" she exclaimed.

She nearly dropped the phone as she walked into her office and came face to face with the largest, most colorful bouquet of roses she'd ever seen. It brought a massive grin to her face. Leela felt loved and wanted.

"What?!" Linda yelled. "What happened? I knew we didn't need to trust that bastard."

"Oh, I'm sorry. My... I just walked into something in my office," Leela stammered.

The pleasant scent that floated throughout the office was intoxicating. Instantly, Leela felt better. She didn't realize how tense was until she'd released some of that trapped stress.

"Well, what the hell is it? Got you screaming like a banshee and carrying on," Linda griped.

Leela rolled her eyes. She moved in close and inhaled. These were the kind of signs that made the guilt sink even deeper. The last few days with her husband had been wonderful. Their evening of dinner and a movie came right on time. Riley had been more attentive, and her decision to focus on their marriage for the next three weeks had been a smart move.

"Hey, Mom, I need to run. Riley just sent me the most beautiful flowers, and I want to thank him before he gets caught up in a late-afternoon meeting."

"What about Big Mama and lunch with that snake?!" Linda yelled.

"He's not a snake and it's gonna have to wait. I need to run; I'll call you later."

"Oh no, Ma'am!"

Leela couldn't care less about her mother's protests. She hadn't forgotten how Linda had thrown her under the bus over lunch with Big Mama. Her mother had a negative disposition, and she expected her to always speak her mind, but at times, the negativity was too much.

Leela ended the call with her mother and dialed her husband. As she snatched the card attached to the bouquet, she sat in the chair and greeted him cheerfully when he answered the phone.

"Hey, Sunshine, what are you so giddy about?" Riley asked.

"Oh, I just wanted to say thank you for..." Leela's voice trailed off when her eyes connected with the words on the card.

The roses were from Malone, not Riley.

Leela's heart threatened to stop and her throat went dry.

"Thank me for what?" Riley asked.

"Uh. I'm sorry. I dunno, um," Leela stammered.

"Leela, what the hell is going on?" Riley asked. His tone had taken a complete turn, and there was nothing friendly about his voice. He sounded pissed and highly irritated.

"Leela!"

"Oh, sorry, Babe, something just... I need to run, I'll call you, or see you later at home."

Had she lost it that much? Why hadn't she checked the card before she assumed her husband had sent the flowers? He hadn't sent flowers to her job in more than seven years! She felt completely frazzled and tongue-tied. Before she stumbled again and put her foot completely in her mouth, she quickly hung up the phone.

Leela released a trapped breath and tried to pull herself together. Nervously, she glanced back at the bouquet. She wanted to hate it, wanted to fight the wonderful feeling that began to wash over her. Malone was making his presence known, and it was becoming more and more difficult to ignore him, like she knew she should.

He's thoughtful, sexy, and considerate too? Did her husband even stand a chance?

"You would need to get there Friday afternoon, because the meeting is at seven forty-five Friday evening. Then the last meeting wraps up early Saturday afternoon around three thirty," Mr. Watson, Riley's boss, said.

Riley felt uncomfortable for the first time in his professional life. He was completely uneasy about the idea of going out of town for three days. He listened as his boss rattled off details about what needed to be accomplished during the trip. Although the trip was a couple of weeks away, he already knew he didn't want to go.

"The papers should be signed before you leave Sunday. We have a meeting first thing Monday morning, so you need to circle back before you leave."

He knew there was nothing he could do about the scheduled trip, but he didn't want to leave his wife at home alone. It wouldn't be a Free Friday weekend, but the thought still made him uncomfortable. There was no way his boss, Mr. Watson, would allow Riley to send someone else in his place. He understood that was nothing but wishful thinking.

After leaving the conference room, Riley strode down the hall and back toward his office.

"Franklin," a colleague greeted as they passed each other in the hall. Riley gave an acknowledging nod and kept moving. His mind was far away from work and the upcoming trip he couldn't avoid.

What would happen if he left his wife home alone for three

entire days? Maybe he was making more out of the situation than necessary. If he didn't trust his own wife, he knew that was a sign that they had major problems.

Riley was disappointed in himself; he had allowed Bill to get in his head and now everything drove him crazy. Six months ago, he didn't have thoughts of his wife being with another man, but everything seemed to change once Bill and Samantha called it quits. Despite knowing that, Riley still allowed his mind to race with crazy thoughts.

He wanted to believe he was right, but his gut told him otherwise. Why had he let Bill talk him into Free Fridays in the first damn place? Better yet, why did he fall for the okie-doke? He didn't have to prove anything to anyone, especially someone who couldn't handle his own household when he was married.

Inside his office, Riley logged on to his computer and checked the itinerary his assistant provided. His travel plans were as good as set in stone.

He picked up the phone and was about to call his wife when he noticed she was already on the line. His plan was to ask her to accompany him on the trip. However, on such short notice, she wouldn't be able to join him even if she wanted. She had to have at least a month's notice for time off, and he had to leave late Thursday night. Besides, if she accompanied him, she'd be bored because the meetings and wining and dining clients.

Riley found their exchange over the phone strange, and he knew this time it wasn't his mind playing tricks. She sounded odd, and with everything that had changed between them, it didn't take much to feed his suspicions.

Riley pushed back his chair, got up and strode around his office. In his mind, he played out several scenarios, but none were good. Finally, he went to his cell phone and dialed Bill.

"What's up?"

"You in the building?" Bill asked. "I was just about to call you."

"Yeah, in my office. Why? You here?" Riley asked.

"Okay, bet that. I'm upstairs, but I'll be there in ten."

In the time it took Bill to come down to Riley's office, Riley had gone back and forth over whether he should discuss his concerns with his friend.

He couldn't remember a time when he had been so insecure and indecisive. What the hell was happening?

"Bill is here to see you," Riley's assistant's voice announced through the speaker on his phone.

"Send him in."

"Aey, Dawg," Bill greeted.

The two bumped fists and managed a half-hug.

"So, when you coming back to work?" Riley asked.

"We're still working out some details, but it's looking good, real good, Man. What's up with you?"

"Gotta head out to Oklahoma City in a couple of weeks," Riley said.

"Damn, why you sound like that about it, Bruh?"

"Here you go with all these damn feelings again," Riley complained. "When you gonna let that go?"

CHAPTER 31

"He is single-handedly changing my view of men. I mean, he's everything Bill was not. Do you know we even talk about other women?"

Leela was bored. All Samantha had been doing the whole time they were at lunch, as they ate, and now afterward, was talk about Kent and how wonderful he was. She was glad that her girl had found someone who had restored her faith in the opposite sex, but did they always have to talk about him?

"Okay, okay, can you look any less interested in my conversation?" Samantha stopped and suddenly asked.

"Oh, no. It's not that. I'm worried; that's all. If it's not problems with Big Mama, it's problems with Riley. I swear, I'm glad Kent is everything you've ever wanted in a man. I promise I am interested, because I can remember several months ago when you had me worried."

"Worried about what?"

"Don't you remember? All that talk about how marriage didn't make sense and how people shouldn't expect to stay together until death."

"Oh, yeah. I do remember all of that. And I still agree to a certain point, but I guess what I should have said is, it takes two people who are right for each other to make it work," Samantha admitted.

Leela nearly fell from her chair. She wasn't about to remind

Samantha of all the crazy things she'd said back then. But it was almost like a completely different woman was talking now. Or that's what she thought until after a moment of silence, Samantha started up again.

"Actually. My position hasn't really changed. I still feel like marriages like your grandparents will soon be a thing of the past. Gone are the years when people get married to their high school sweetheart and they remain happily married until their golden years and beyond."

Leela raised an eyebrow.

"Hear me out. You've seen TV shows when the couple is old and have been married for many, many years."

"Yeah?"

"Do you ever notice how grumpy they are? Often the man can't find a single nice thing to say about his wife; the wife is frustrated, has long lost that loving feeling, is tired of picking up behind him and she's exhausted."

Leela's head tilted ever so slightly.

"Leela, they're miserable, and in most cases, they've made most people around them miserable too. I'm not saying that's the case with all of the couples, but for the majority of them, it is. Now, if those same people looked at each other, ten, maybe even fifteen years in and decided they no longer made each other happy being together, they could've gone their separate ways and still remained friends."

Samantha shrugged and clapped her hands as if to say she's finished and proven her point. "However, I will say I enjoy my time with Kent, and he makes me happy. Now, for as long as I make him happy and he's happy with me, we'll see where it goes."

"Maybe marriage one day?" Leela asked cautiously.

"Nah. Not my cup of tea. I won't say I'll never do it again, but

I can say I'm not looking for happily ever after forever." Samantha smiled. "But, I do think we might be the right combination."

They had finished lunch and were just talking. Leela felt like Samantha looked happy, so maybe she was on to something. Maybe it did take the right combination to make the difference in marriage.

The more she thought about it, the more she wondered whether she and Riley had ever been the right combination. She also thought about what life would be like if she was married to Malone instead.

"Will you ladies be needing anything else? Dessert maybe?" the waiter asked.

"None for me," Samantha quickly responded.

"Me either," Leela added.

The waiter removed the check from his apron and placed it on the table. "Whenever you're ready," he said and walked away.

After he left, Leela leaned in and whispered, "I've got a major problem, and I don't know what to do about it."

"Oh, what's wrong? And here I am blabbing on and on about me and Kent and everything that's so wonderful, and you've got something going on. I'm sorry, Sweetness," Samantha said.

They burst out laughing.

"You need to quit," Leela said. "I'm being serious."

"Okay, Honey. I'm sorry. What's the problem?"

"I think I'm falling in love with another man."

Samantha's eyes grew wide.

"See, why you gotta be so silly? I'm being serious!"

"I'm not being silly. I'm really stunned. I'm stunned that you finally admitted it."

Leela smiled awkwardly. That's exactly what she had done. She'd finally admitted aloud what she had known for quite some time. The problem was, she didn't feel like there was much she could do about her problem.

Samantha reached for her hand across the table. "Don't worry, Sweetness, admitting the problem is the first step toward a solution."

Despite what her love-struck friend said, Leela knew there was no amicable solution to her problem. Riley would blow a gasket if he ever thought she was interested in another man. Free Friday or not, she knew her husband and what he would or would not tolerate.

"We should do something special for the next Free Friday," Samantha suggested.

Leela rolled her eyes. That's what had gotten her into trouble in the first damn place.

"And let me guess, by something special, you mean the four of us on a double-date," Leela said.

Samantha pursed her lips, but Leela was still able to see the smile that lingered on her face. "Listen, I believe in the right combination. And I know you don't wanna hear this, but Malone and you…that's a good strong combination."

That wasn't what Leela wanted to hear. Regardless of whether it was true, it wasn't what she wanted to hear.

The days seemed to pass in a flash. Leela carried her secret as she went about her daily routine, and for the most part, life seemed normal.

Throughout the day, she'd get loving text messages on her phone from Mary, and they always brought a smile to her face. Then by the time her day ended, she felt like she had to drag herself home to Riley.

Once there, she never really knew what to expect. Riley's behavior had gone through so many changes, Leela felt like each evening was an experience with a new man.

"Hey, I need to go out of town on business next week," he said once she walked in and found him in the kitchen.

"Okay. Where are you going?"

"Oklahoma City. I'll be gone Wednesday through Friday."

"Okay, thanks for letting me know."

"Oh, and I picked up Chinese food; had a yen for it."

Leela nodded as she watched him put food in a glass dish. "I'm gonna go change and clean up before I eat."

When she left the kitchen, he was stuffing his face, and she didn't know if he even heard what she'd said.

Thoughts of Malone were never far from her mind. At this point, Leela felt like she and Riley were simply going through the motions. She thought about the conversation she'd had with Big Mama. Her grandmother had been faithful and devoted to her grandfather all those years and look at what she got.

Life was too short to second-guess something as important as the person you're sharing it with. The things that she hated most about Riley were nothing new; he hadn't changed. But maybe she had. She used to think of his bossy ways as a sign of his affection, but at times it felt like it was borderline abuse.

Before Malone came along, she hadn't thought about a relationship where she was treated as an equal. Now, she was scrutinizing everything about her life with Riley.

Leela took a hot shower and fantasized about being with Malone. After the shower, she changed into lounge wear and returned to the kitchen.

Everything was dark. Her husband must've been tucked away in his cave watching a game. Once she flicked on the light, she pulled out the containers and fixed herself a plate.

"Isn't it a little late for you to be eating?"

Leela's head whipped around to her husband. He was putting a beer bottle into the recycling bin and pulling the refrigerator door open. He dipped into the ice box and pulled out another beer. "What took you so long to make it home anyway?"

"Was I late or something?"

She knew what he thought before he verbalized it.

"When did you start doing shit just because you know it bothers me?"

Leela's forehead wrinkled at his accusation. She wasn't sure how to respond because the last thing she wanted was a fight. "The 'answer a question with a question' thing?"

"It's not just that. Something is going on with you. It's like you're starting to smell yourself, like the old people would say."

His comment stung.

"I'm hungry, so I'm gonna finish eating before my food gets cold."

"When was the last time we had sex?"

Leela nearly choked on the forkful she'd placed in her mouth.

It must've been a rhetorical question because Riley snapped the cap from his bottle and took a swig as he walked out of the kitchen. He didn't wait for an answer, nor did he wait to see if anything was caught in his wife's throat.

CHAPTER 32

"This is an emergency and I need you to drop whatever you're doing and come meet me at Big Mama's apartment now!"

The demand from her mother didn't instantly sound an alarm with Leela. She was sick and tired of everyone pushing her around. It didn't matter whether she was at home, at the office, or on the phone with relatives, just about everyone in her life felt like they could pass out marching orders, and she should get to stepping. Leela was fed up.

"Mom, I need you to calm down." Leela felt the calmer she remained, the more likely her mother would follow her lead. But she should've known better. Linda always exploded without any concern for others.

"Calm down, hell! She has lost all of her common sense and I'm not gonna stand for it. You'd better make your way over there or I swear for God, somebody is going to jail today!"

Leela hated when Linda huffed and made all kinds of threats when she didn't get her way. Her mother needed a man! That's exactly what she needed. If she had a man of her own, maybe she wouldn't be so stressed and wound so tightly all the time.

"Mom," Leela called into the phone again.

When she realized Linda had hung up, she finished the email she was typing, then hit the buzzer that connected her to her assistant.

"Hey, something has come up. I need to take off early. Please let anyone who's looking for me know I can be reached on my cell until five."

"Okay. Is everything all right?"

"Yes. It's my grandmother again. Thanks for asking."

Leela left the office and strolled out to her car. She knew she probably needed to be a bit more concerned than she was, but her mother was a drama queen, with a knack for exaggerating.

By the time she got behind the wheel and left the parking lot, Linda had already called back three times. Leela wanted to remind her that she was the one who had hung up the phone, but she knew not to add any fuel when Linda was hot.

"Where are you?" Linda barked into the phone.

"I'm on my way. Now, do you care to tell me what's going on?"

"Oh, I'll tell you all right. What's going on is somebody is about to go to jail. I'm sick of this mess. Big Mama is over here talking like she done forgot what that bastard did, and I'm not about to sit by and let that happen."

Leela blew out a breath. She should've known, but she decided she'd remain calm and try to hold Linda on the phone for as long as possible. There was no need for anyone to go to jail.

Nearly twenty minutes later, Leela pulled up at her grandmother's complex and was shocked to see her mother pacing back and forth in the parking lot. For all of the talking Linda had done, she thought she'd been inside the apartment with Big Mama, and in need of physical restraint.

"Hey, Ma, what's going on?" Leela asked as she approached. She intentionally kept her tone calm and soft.

Linda looked exasperated. She put out the cigarette she was puffing on, and blew out a plume of smoke. She had stopped smoking too many times to count.

"Chile, wait until you hear this one! I swear, some women make me wanna...ugh!"

Without much of an explanation, Linda all but dragged Leela up to Big Mama's apartment, where she burst into the place without knocking on the front door.

"Okay, now, tell her what you told me," Linda challenged Big Mama.

Beverly sighed and put down the glass she had washed at the sink. She walked around to the front of the counter and wiped her hands on a dish cloth.

"Why did you drag this chile over here?" Beverly looked at Leela. "You didn't have to work today?"

Leela looked at her mother, then back at her grandmother. "I was at work when she called me, going ballistic, so I left work early and rushed over."

Linda's eyes darted around the apartment like she was looking for something. It wasn't until the toilet flushed that Leela realized they weren't alone. All eyes turned toward the hall when the bathroom door opened.

Linda threw her arms up in the air and huffed loudly. "Tell her!" she screamed at her mother.

"Tell me what?" Leela asked.

"Your mother is upset because I've decided to let your grandfather move in here."

Linda threw her hands to her hips and started tapping one foot. Now the focus was on Leela. Leela was a bit surprised, but she wasn't all torn up like her mother. She actually thought it made sense. The two had been married for more than fifty years. Apart, they simply weren't any good. Since the two had reconciled, Big Mama hadn't been back to the hospital.

"And what do you want me to do about this?" Leela asked her mother. She still spoke calmly.

"You, we, somebody needs to talk some sense into her! That no-good bastard can't live here!"

Suddenly, something happened that no one expected. Linda broke down and cried. While Leela and Big Mama were too stunned to move, it was her grandfather who walked over and took his daughter into his arms. He held her like she was a little child.

"Baby, I am so sorry. I am sorry for hurting you, hurting our family and letting you down. I know I have hurt you, and if I knew how to make any of that pain go away, I would've made it vanish a long time ago."

There wasn't a dry eye in the apartment.

Normally, Leela would have rushed to call Riley and tell him everything that happened at her grandmother's house. But as she walked to the car and ended one of the most emotional days she'd experienced, she found herself desperate to get Malone on the phone.

"Oh, Sweetness, she's been hurting and she didn't know what to do with her pain, that's all," Malone said.

"Yeah, but you'd have to know my mother to know how absolutely out of character that was for her. She's the one who has always told everyone else what to do. She's bullied us for so long, we just thought she was the strongest."

"Well, even the strongest take a fall," he said. "We're vulnerable too."

Leela knew he was right. It was good to see her mother finally talking to her grandfather. The relationship between the two was finally on a path of mending.

"So, Sweetness, do you have to rush back home?"

The thought never crossed her mind until he asked. Excitement flushed through her veins. There was something so enticing about doing what she knew was wrong. She'd been drawn to trouble like it was second nature.

"Not really. Why? What'd you have in mind?"

"We can meet somewhere for a little while, maybe just to have a quick drink? I just want to see you."

He was so sweet.

"Okay, let's meet somewhere. Where do you think?"

"You've gotta go back to Katy, so we can meet somewhere along I-10. That way, you'll be closer to home. There's a Chili's over there, Pappasito's, or we can pick a parking lot. Let me know."

Nearly an hour later, the windows inside Leela's car were fogged up like that of two teenagers parked at Lover's Lane.

She couldn't control her breathing, and Malone couldn't keep his hands off of her.

"How much time do you have?" he asked in between two hot, steamy kisses.

"I don't know. I'm not really on a time schedule, but I don't want to raise any flags, either."

"Yes. That's smart. But I was thinking maybe we could go get a room for a couple of hours."

Leela's expression told him all he needed to know.

"Sorry, but it was worth a try, right?"

Malone adjusted his body in the seat.

They kissed again. And again, Malone's hand found its way under her blouse and into her bra. He flicked her stiffened nipple, and she enjoyed the way it felt. But this time, Leela allowed her hands to do some exploring too.

She traveled to his crotch and squeezed the hardness that bulged through his jeans.

The windows were still fogged up.

"I'd better go."

"Yes. You should. We've gotta stop," Malone said.

They kissed one last time. It was long, wet, and sloppy, and Leela couldn't get enough.

When her cell phone rang, she finally pulled back and forced Malone to get out of the car so she could go home. It was Linda.

Leela answered, "Hey, Ma, I need a few minutes. I'll call you back."

She quickly rolled down the window and called Malone.

"What's the matter?" Leela asked.

He stopped when she called out to him, but he didn't turn around.

"Malone, you okay?"

She saw his massive back move, and noticed when he pulled in a deep breath. He turned around and approached the car.

"You wanna really know what's wrong?"

Leela looked up at him and struggled to contain the feelings that were washing over her. Slowly, she nodded.

"Everything is wrong. Absolutely everything, Sweetness. You think I like having to meet up with you and watch the clock? You tell me that fool talks to you like he owns you. I have to settle for a few stolen moments here or there or I have to wait until the last Friday of the month. Listen, I know I said I could handle this. I thought I could, but I'm not so sure anymore."

Leela swallowed the lump in her dry throat.

"I'm sorry. I've been trying my best to keep this to myself. I shouldn't have said anything, and I wouldn't have. I thought you were leaving."

Leela eased the door open and got out of the car. Malone stepped back to give her space.

She jumped into his arms and squeezed him as tightly as she could. "I am so sorry to do this to you. I am so sorry, Babe. I know you're absolutely right. We can't go on like this; we can't. I just need some time. I need to sort this out."

Malone averted his eyes, but kept his hands on her. Leela used her hand to touch his chin and turn his face to hers. She looked up and into his eyes. Once she focused in on his eyes, she noticed they were filled with tears.

They kissed again and again.

CHAPTER 33

The last time Riley had gone out of town on business and Samantha came over, things were different. Leela's mind was nearly overwhelmed with thoughts of just how much had changed, as she sat on the bed Thursday evening, and watched her husband pack. Was she excited to see him go because of Malone?

"What's on your mind over there? What's up with you?" Riley asked.

"I'm fine; why you ask?"

Man, was she that obvious? Could he sense another man? Was he able to smell Malone's scent on her?

"What'd I tell you about answering a question with a question?" Riley said, as he stuffed underwear and socks into a side pocket of his large leather travel bag.

Leela shook her head. "I said I'm fine. That's not a question."

Riley looked at her with tight lips as he moved to the dresser for T-shirts. "I'm fine, why you ask? Sounds like a question to me."

Leela rolled her eyes and then instantly regretted the move. She felt relieved when she realized he wasn't paying attention and missed the move.

"What do you plan to do with yourself while I'm gone?" he asked.

"What do I always do when you travel? The same thing I do when you're here. What do you mean?"

Riley didn't say anything; he gave her a knowing look before he slipped into the closet. He didn't need to say a word for her to realize the mistake she had made. She felt relief when he lingered in the closet. He emerged with two blazers and a pair of boots.

"You know I don't want your friend here while I'm gone." Riley started to close the bag. "As a matter of fact, I don't even want you with her."

Leela couldn't believe her ears. He couldn't be serious. She waited for him to retract his comment or even clarify his words, but he didn't.

"So, you're not gonna say anything? Did you hear what I said? I don't want Samantha over here while I'm gone, and I damn sure don't want you with her," he repeated. "You need to go spend some time with Big Mama."

"I'm not a child, Ry. If I want to see Samantha or want her over here, she should be able to come, and the fact that you suddenly don't like her, doesn't mean I'm about to treat her differently."

"This ain't up for discussion and we damn sure not about to debate it. I'm the man of this house, and if I don't want my wife slutting around with someone, I should be able to say that. Now last time I checked, what I wanted mattered to you." Riley's tone had changed and there was nothing friendly about it.

Leela couldn't believe they were battling over Samantha. She was about to fire back at him, but caught herself. In less than an hour, he would climb into his car and drive to the airport. He'd be gone for an entire two days. She didn't need to argue with him about what would happen while he was gone. She was quickly beginning to agree that what her husband didn't know, wouldn't hurt him, nor stress her.

"You got me?" Riley asked.

Reluctant to answer, Leela struggled to mask her expression. She hated when he went all cave-man, barbaric, Neanderthal on her.

Leela wondered why he couldn't figure it out, but she was tired of trying to explain to him how he should treat his wife.

"Leela, I'm serious. I don't want you with that bitch, and I don't want her over here while I'm gone. She ain't welcome here anymore and I mean that. You got it?"

"Are you done yet? And before you go on about me answering a question with a question, let's just drop it, okay? Samantha ain't interested in coming over here, so you're wasting your energy for nothing. Can't you just let it rest?"

"There you go again. Man, if you could only stop answering my questions with questions. But yeah, okay, she ain't interested because she knows I'm here," Riley said. "I want you to stay away from her."

Leela got up and walked out of the room. She was done with the conversation, but it seemed like her husband refused to take the hint.

As far as Leela was concerned, her husband couldn't hit the road fast enough.

Riley considered himself to be a lot of things, but stupid wasn't one of them. He realized his marriage was in danger long before his wife understood what was going on. He blamed Samantha for a lot of what had changed in Leela, but he also knew there was a great deal he couldn't blame on anyone but himself.

Karma was a bitch. That's what he thought as he accepted a call from Bill.

"You on your way to the airport?" Bill asked.

"Yeah, what's up?"

"Hold on a sec," Bill said.

Riley pulled into the airport garage. He wasn't prepared for the voice he heard next in his ear.

"Why are you ignoring my calls?" Natasha asked.

There was far too much on his mind to add Natasha to the list. She was just as needy as ever and he hated when Bill continued to feed her hope.

"Natasha, what's up?"

Riley tried to make his voice sound like he was rushing. He hoped she'd take the hint and not keep him on the phone.

"You. That's what I'm trying to tell you, Ry. Stop fighting it. I'm not going to cause any problems for you. I just want some of your time. Bill tells me you're traveling for work. If I'd known, I could've come with you, Baby," she purred.

For a second, what she said sounded good, not because she'd take the trip with him, but because she obviously felt he was important enough to want to tag along, unlike his wife.

"We know that wouldn't have worked," Riley said.

He was getting tired of Natasha and her constant pressure. But the one who pissed him off even more was Bill. Riley couldn't understand why his friend didn't shut Natasha down before she got to him; instead, he encouraged her.

"Hey, listen, I need to park and get to my gate. I'm running kind of late."

"But I just got on the phone with you; can't we talk until you have to go through security?" she begged.

Riley rolled his eyes.

"Nah, Natasha. I have Clear. That means I won't have to stand in line; I'll breeze through security and pre-board when I get to my gate. I'll have to catch up with you later. Tell Bill I'll holler." Riley was about to hang up until she yelled.

"But wait!" Natasha said.

"No, I gotta run." This time, he didn't wait for her to respond, nor did he try to listen to whatever it was she wanted him to wait to hear. He hung up the phone and found a parking spot.

Riley arrived at the airport with time to spare. He parked on the lower level of the parking structure and walked into the terminal. He planned to sit at a bar and throw back a few drinks before he made his way over to his gate.

After he breezed through security and settled onto a bar stool, he checked out the many games that were on display. Then he dug his iPad out of his bag. His eyes followed the green dot that was on the move.

"Women can be so damn hard-headed," he muttered, as he watched the dot travel along a familiar route. Riley sipped his drink and started to think about how he was going to handle the biggest dilemma he faced. Why was she out so late? She had to go to work in the morning.

Free Fridays were not going the way he expected, and he had to figure out whether he should approach his wife about what was next.

A nagging feeling told Riley this was the worst time possible to be leaving town.

CHAPTER 34

In the years Leela had been with Riley, he rarely sent anything to the office. But Malone had already sent two beautiful bouquets of roses, and she wanted to let him know how thoughtful she thought he was.

"Yes! They were beautiful. I don't know what I'm going to do with you," Leela said sweetly into the phone as she drove.

"Sweetness, you can do whatever you like. I just hope you do it often and you enjoy it too," Malone said.

They laughed at his lewd inside joke. Leela found herself laughing much more in his presence, when they talked, or even when she thought about him. Those were the kinds of feelings she used to have for her husband.

Guilt. Again. It seemed to follow her like a persistent shadow.

"So how much time do we have together tonight?" Malone asked. Before Leela could answer, he quickly added, "Samantha said she was gonna set something up; you game, right?"

Leela was tempted to say no. There was a small part of her that wanted to decline, but she wouldn't mean it. She had to be honest with herself, regardless of how hard she struggled to live the lie.

"I haven't talked to her yet." Leela wondered if he picked up on her attempt to stall. After their last meeting in the parking lot, she really struggled to get off the fence. She wished she could wave a magic wand and uncomplicate her life.

"You don't have to talk to her to know that I want to see you, so what's up?"

He didn't give up easily. She liked that about him, but more importantly, she liked the way he treated her and spoke *to* her, instead of *at* her. That was something Riley couldn't stop doing.

The way her husband had gone on and on about Samantha not being allowed to come to the house while he was gone, she wondered whether he knew she was not a kid.

"I know your man is gone for a few days, but I'm not gonna pressure you because I want you to be comfortable. All I'm gonna add is, this would be a great chance for us to spend some uninterrupted time together."

Leela was mad at the butterflies that insistently came to life in the pit of her stomach. How could she be so giddy with excitement over the suggestion of something so wrong?

"Ah, I'm not sure about that."

"Sweetness, that's what you're telling me, but I know for a fact, your face, your heart even, is telling a different story."

"I can't, Malone. You know I can't," she whined.

"It sounds to me like you want to, and I want you to, so what's stopping you? He's gone, right?"

"Yes."

"Well, Sweetness, let's do this. I wanna wake up with you next to me. I want you to wake up in my arms. Imagine, we can spend the evening eating strawberries, sipping champagne, and acting like an old married couple."

Leela laughed.

"I can tell you've never been married," she joked.

"Why? What's that supposed to mean?" Malone feigned that he was insulted.

"Well, for one thing, old married people don't sit around sipping champagne."

"See, that's where you're wrong. If you were my wife, we'd sip champagne on a regular, Baby, and we'd damn sure celebrate each other often."

He always knew what to say.

Life suddenly stopped for Riley as he stood in the middle of the busy airport terminal. He was at his gate.

"I have an emergency and I need to talk to Mr. Watson," Riley said into his cell phone.

He was more than upset as he stood and waited. His eyes darted around the busy gate. Blood rushed through his veins so fast, he literally felt like he was on speed. A thin layer of sweat blanketed his forehead and the back of his neck. He tried to calm himself as he waited for the person on the other end to verify the information he'd just received.

Nothing moved as fast as he needed.

"Hi, Riley. We are aware of the situation. Mr. Watson is on the other line now, trying to salvage details of the deal. Please stand by," his boss's assistant said into the phone.

Moments before Riley was about to board the plane, he received a frantic message from his own assistant. He was frustrated because he never wanted to go in the first place.

"Thank God, you're not on the plane yet. The meeting needs to be postponed; there's been a horrible accident."

Riley ended the call with her and quickly dialed his boss's office. The problem was, boarding for the flight had started and business passengers were already walking onto the plane.

"Is there any news on the meeting? They're boarding the flight now," he said as soon as his boss's assistant answered.

"Yes, Riley. I was just about to call you. The meeting has been rescheduled due to an emergency. You are not required to make the trip. So sorry for the inconvenience."

Riley sighed. "Okay. Thanks. I'll be in the office tomorrow."

When he ended the call, he started to call home to let Leela know, but then he decided to call Bill first.

Thoughts of Natasha entered his head and he decided against that too. It was a damn shame that he had to think twice before he could place a call.

Riley made his way back through the crowded airport with lots of thoughts racing through his mind. He could go into the office or finish up from home. He decided the change in plans would be a great surprise for Leela. Lately, his active imagination had wreaked havoc on his marriage. He wanted the evidence to be wrong.

For her part, Leela hadn't done anything to make him think she was being unfaithful, but the thing with Bill had nearly pushed him over the edge. When he thought logically, he understood this was nothing more than Bill trying to reclaim their youthful single days, but there was still that part of him that felt like his manhood was being challenged.

Back at his car and behind the wheel, Riley decided against going into the office tomorrow. He'd go home and surprise his wife. It would still be early enough for a nice romantic dinner; they could make love, and plan to play hooky together on Friday. They needed some quiet, alone time. He was so upset with her that he didn't even get any before he left for the trip.

It was about time he tried to put some romance back into their marriage. The more he thought about it, the more he realized that lately his paranoia had caused them to behave more like two people who shared living space but not much else.

He was tired, and he knew it was about time he made some changes.

Riley merged onto Beltway 8 and eased into one of the middle lanes. As he fidgeted with the radio, he looked up in time to see a sea of red taillights ahead. Traffic had come to a sudden stop.

He quickly increased the volume and listened in horror.

A massive 18-wheeler accident closed down all lanes of the freeway. So, instead of getting home to try and salvage the night, he'd be stuck in gridlock traffic for hours.

"Damn! Could this crap get any worse?"

Nearly three hours later, Riley tried to tell himself to ignore the image he had seen on his iPad. After spending hours in traffic, he wanted nothing more than to go home and do the right thing. He wanted to go home and wait on his wife. He knew she had left for Samantha's house, but quite surely she wasn't gonna stay there all night.

The romantic dinner idea had seemed like the perfect thing to do, but that was before the 18-wheeler accident on the freeway. That was before bumper-to-bumper frustration had gotten the best of him.

People had cut off their engines and started to mingle right there on the highway, but he wanted no part of that. He wanted to get home to his wife. He needed to put eyes on her.

Once traffic started moving again, Riley called Bill.

He was so pissed that the minute Leela thought he was gone, she went off and did her own thing. Now he knew for sure, his suspicions must be valid.

Once he got Bill on the phone and told him everything, Bill seemed worried.

"Don't do nothing stupid, Dawg," Bill warned Riley. "She ain't worth it, Man. Believe that!" He sighed. "I know you pissed, 'cause you told her to stay away from there, but try to calm down, Dawg."

The situation wasn't completely lost on Riley. He remembered months ago when their roles were reversed. It was him talking Bill off the ledge. He had sworn it would never happen to him; he wore the pants in his house and not a day had gone by that he didn't let Leela know.

"If anything is going on, I'm gonna kill her, man," Riley said.

The iPad he used to track his wife's movements had been stuck at Samantha's address the whole time he'd been stuck in traffic. She had defied his orders, and the minute she thought he was gone and she was alone, she'd proven that he could no longer trust her to do the right thing. What really pissed him off was the fact that Leela did exactly what he'd told her not to do. He was fed up and he was not about to let this shit slide.

He ended the call with Bill; he didn't need to be talked out of anything. All he needed was to find his wife, and for her sake, he prayed the slut would be the only person she was with when he finally arrived.

CHAPTER 35

With music softly playing, her lips were gently saying, "Maaalone, pleease, stop. I can't."

But when a thick chocolate finger fumbled into her mouth, she sucked and suckled.

Leela breathed hard and struggled to fight the pure bliss she felt. Her brain raced with thoughts of how something that felt so good, could be so very wrong. Her insides tingled as if every single nerve in her body had been ignited. He moved his hand from her mouth.

"Please, Malone."

She painstakingly begged for mercy, and urged him to stop, but her body moved in sync with his, like she enjoyed everything he was doing.

"Oh, God!"

She was writhing in agony, as if she wanted to get away.

But she was no match for Malone's strength. Pinned in the corner of a soft leather sofa, there was no way for Leela to escape. She bit down on her bottom lip as Malone adjusted her hips and positioned her thighs over his shoulders. He was on his knees, with his head buried between her legs.

Leela's body squirmed, but he wouldn't let up. When she felt his strong and steady fingers stroke her inner thighs, she thought she'd died and gone to heaven.

Instinctively, she gyrated and moved to a rhythm that was slow and deliberate. Malone's soft tongue flickered tenderly against her swollen, hypersensitive clit and nearly brought tears of pleasure to her eyes.

She felt the sensation as it slowly built and traveled up her weakened legs. Everything he said and did felt good. His words made her cream without trying; his touch was electrifying, and dazzled every spot on her skin.

They'd been alone while Kent and Samantha went shopping for dessert. The guys had grilled steaks and lobster tails, but there was nothing for dessert, so Kent and Samantha decided to make a run. That left Leela alone with Malone

"You guys coming to the store or staying here?" Samantha had asked.

Leela had eyed Malone, but neither answered.

The seductive grin on their faces told the entire story.

"Okay then. We'll be back," Samantha had said. "Don't do anything I wouldn't do."

Leela remained resolved to set some ground rules for Malone. They couldn't go on the way they had been; it wouldn't be good for anyone.

"We need to talk," she had said.

Malone had gotten close. She'd smelled his scent and felt his breath as he got closer.

One minute Leela was explaining why she needed to back off and give her marriage a chance; then the next, her panties were coming off and Malone was adjusting himself between her thighs.

"I need a taste before dessert."

"No, Malone, this is not a good idea."

"Let me taste you. Let me make you feel good, help take the edge off. Your mind is somewhere else. I want you here with me."

Leela knew he was right. She'd been deep in thought. The battle that brewed in her head began the moment they arrived at Samantha's.

Malone eased back slightly and gazed down at her. His eyes took in every inch of her womanhood. He removed his shirt and yanked off the skirt she wore.

She had given up. There was no point in fighting anymore. She gave in. She allowed herself to let go of all hesitation and simply enjoy what was happening. Her body was already there. Her heart left first; now, she just needed to release herself mentally and enjoy.

"Let's go to the back, so we can be comfortable," Malone said as he pulled back from the work he was doing between her thighs.

Breathing hard and heavy, Leela couldn't find her voice, but she wanted to go. She wanted to follow him regardless of the consequences. She needed him to go back to what he had been doing moments earlier. She fought the urge to grab his head in her hands and guide him back to where he had been.

There was no turning back, was there?

When the hurried knock sounded at the door, a sense of relief washed over Leela. She had gone too far; they had done too much. The interruption had come right on time.

"The door," she whispered. "Samantha probably forgot something; go get it."

"Then we'll go to the back?" Malone asked.

"Yes."

Leela scrambled for her panties and her skirt. Eager and anxious, Malone rushed to the door and pulled it open. But the sound of a question from the door stopped Leela cold in her tracks.

"Where the hell is my wife?"

Riley?

Leela couldn't move a single muscle. There she was, in the middle of her best friend's living room, naked from the waist down, with her panties in one hand, and her skirt in the other, and caught between her lover and her husband.

At first, when Samantha saw Bill's number flash across her screen, instinct told her to ignore the call. She still had nothing to discuss with him and thought it odd that he'd call.

She turned to Kent and smirked. "Can you believe the nerve? My loser ex is calling."

Kent's eyebrows went up.

"It ain't nothing like that. Actually, Babe, I'm wondering whether someone died or something. He has absolutely no reason whatsoever to call me." She shrugged and put the phone back into her purse.

"Well, answer and find out what he wants."

"You don't mind?"

"Why would I? I'm not worried," Kent said and playfully smacked her on the behind.

Before she could answer, the phone stopped ringing.

Samantha shrugged again, and they moved on to the next aisle in the grocery store.

"You guys want wine or something stronger. I could get some of those frozen mixes."

"Nah. We'd better stick with wine. I don't want to scare Leela."

They laughed at that and Samantha went to select a bottle. She picked a couple of Chardonnays and brought them back to the basket.

The moment she placed them down, her phone began to ring again.

"It's him again." Samantha showed the phone as if to prove he was calling back.

"Get it."

Samantha stopped, and picked up the phone. "Hello?" There was not a trace of enthusiasm or excitement in her voice. She actually sounded kind of disturbed.

"Yo, Sam, where you at?" Bill asked.

Samantha frowned. His cheerful voice and question left her confused. "My days of answering to you ended a long time ago," she hissed.

She was surprised at the amount of animosity she still held for him. Kent walked farther down the aisle, and she appreciated it. She didn't need him to witness just how nasty she could get; Bill was definitely about to take her there.

"Listen. I'm only asking because I think Riley is about to go ham on your girl. I just wanted to know whether she was with you or not, that's all."

"What do you mean he's about to go ham on my girl? I thought he was out of town. He's supposed to be gone for a few days, isn't he?" Samantha felt panic flood her system.

"He was, but his trip was cancelled. I think he went by the house and when she wasn't there, he got pissed. Said something about heading over to your place. Look, I'm only calling because I don't need my boy to catch a case."

Dread settled in quickly. Samantha thought about the lust she had witnessed in her friend's eyes as they left the two alone. Riley's presence would only cause problems.

"Okay, um. Thanks for the heads-up. I need to run."

"Wait. Sam, what y'all up to? Do I need to come over there?" Bill asked.

Samantha didn't answer as she rushed toward Kent. The frantic look in her eyes told him something wasn't right.

"What happened? What did he say?"

"We need to go. We don't have time for this. Like we need to go *now.* Riley is headed to my place."

"Riley? I thought he was outta town."

"He was, or was supposed to be, but something happened and his trip was cancelled. C'mon; we need to get back to the house."

"Shit. You don't think ol' boy would do anything stupid, do you?" Kent asked.

"Well, considering how much he hates me now and how he warned her to stay away from me, I don't want to take any chances."

They left the basket, its contents, and rushed out of the store.

On the drive back to the house, Kent tried to keep Samantha calm. He discussed all of the reasons Bill's call might have been an overreaction. As he drove, he clutched her hand tightly.

Samantha heard every word he said, and although she appreciated his efforts, the sinking feeling deep in her stomach told her things would not end right.

"I would feel awful if something happened to her. She was very reluctant to hang, but I convinced her that it would be fine."

"C'mon, Baby. Don't beat yourself up. You had no way of knowing dude wasn't gonna leave. I believe dude got some sense; he's not about to do anything stupid. Besides, Malone is there; she's good."

Kent was driving twenty miles over the speed limit, but to Samantha, it still didn't feel fast enough. She picked up the phone and called Leela.

When there was no answer, she picked up Kent's phone and called Malone. When he didn't answer, either, her heart began to race uncontrollably. Samantha wanted them there; she wanted to jump between Riley and Leela and make sure nothing went down.

By the time Kent finally pulled up at her place, she jumped out of the car before he came to a complete stop.

Samantha could hear the loud shouting match as she approached her walkway. Before she made it to the door, Bill's car careened around the corner and screeched to a sudden stop.

"What the hell?!" Samantha screamed at the sight of Bill and a woman as they stormed up the walkway.

The front door was wide open.

The sound of Leela yelling pulled everyone's attention toward the house.

CHAPTER 36

"The jig is up! So I'm the fool is what you're trying to tell me?!" Leela screamed. She couldn't make sense of what had unfolded right before her eyes.

"It wasn't supposed to go down like this. You were supposed to do the right thing. You were supposed to tell him you were married. I didn't think you'd fall for…"

Slap!

Leela couldn't believe she'd swung on her husband until after she'd pulled her arm back and was swinging in the opposite direction.

Slap!

The second and hardest slap of all was reserved for Malone.

"So you were playing me all along?" Tears welled up in her eyes. "Screw you both!"

She slipped on her skirt and was about to storm out until a crowd rushed through the front door. Leela was dumbfounded.

"Bill? And Natasha?"

Leela turned and looked back at Riley. "What the hell is really going on here?"

"You told her, Dawg?" Bill asked.

Riley nodded.

"Man. What's she doing here?" Riley motioned toward Natasha.

"She was with me when you called," Bill said.

"So you brought her here? What gives, Man? What the hell is

up with the two of you? I don't get it. It's like you're working together or something. When is this shit gonna stop?"

Natasha moved forward. "I'm trying to tell you. We were meant to be together. She's not right for you. Look, all it took was another man saying all the right things, and she tossed your vows to the side like they meant nothing. How much longer are you going to deny what you know is true?"

"Natasha, I've already told you. What we had was in the past," Riley said.

"But after I did all of this for you, for us? You still don't want to explore the possibilities with me?"

"You did what? What are you talking about?" Riley asked.

Leela was more than a little upset, but instead of going off the way she wanted to, she fell back and watched the scene unfold. She wasn't sure whom she could trust, but it seemed like Natasha was about to answer lots of questions.

Natasha waved her hands about again.

"All of this. I did it all for you. I set Kelly onto Bill, because I could see it in his eyes; his life needed some adventure. Then, did you think Bill came up with Free Fridays by himself?" Natasha chuckled. "He's just a man. You guys don't think like that. It was me. I came up with the plan. I did it all, so that you could see once and for all that it should've been me all along."

Riley frowned. He looked at Bill, who looked away.

"What's she talking about, Man?"

"I would've...I mean. I thought the idea was cool. She might have come up with it, but I wanted to see what was gonna happen too," Bill stammered. But suddenly, his head turned as if the words had finally sunk in. "You said Kelly? You know her?"

"Bill. Bill. I have to admit, I had no idea the plan would go the way it did, but the signs were there all along. If your marriage was stable with her, no woman would've been able to infiltrate it. Kelly and her husband enjoy an open marriage; you and yours, well, that was just collateral damage. No offense."

Bill stood speechless and dumbfounded.

"So, lemme get this straight," Leela began. "You"—she pointed a finger at Natasha—"You convinced this one to convince this one to approach me about Free Fridays?"

Natasha laughed.

"Oh, how simple you all are. Darlin', once Bill was single, I told Bill that his life would be far better if his best friend was single, too. Men are just that simple. They yearn for the good ol' days, when they were single and sowing their oats. Like I said, it all started with Kelly, and once she did her part, that was just the beginning. No, this was a well-calculated plan."

Natasha inched away from Bill. "See, once that was in motion, I had to set it up so that Kent here and Samantha could meet up. Then, of course, his trusty sidekick, Malone, would need a friend too, and once that was in place, bam!" Natasha slapped her palms together.

"I simply helped Bill see how advantageous it would be if we knocked ol' Riley down a notch or two."

"What's wrong with you?" Leela asked.

Natasha's eyes widened. She pointed at her own chest. "What's wrong with me? Nothing! I'd say my plan was brilliant; I've waited years for this to all come together. I'm patient, and I am determined. I mean, look at where we are now. You're fucking him; he's fucking me; and I think we should just leave things as they are."

"So, you're fucking her?" Leela turned to Riley and asked.

He shook his head saying no.

"It's okay, Daddy. I've been trying to tell you all along, she's moved on. Emotionally, your marriage is over. By now, Malone probably has her eating out of his hands. He's a master at seduction. I hand-picked him myself."

Leela turned to Malone. She had no words.

"Bill, Dawg, how could you do this to me, Man?"

"It's not all she's making it out to be. I'm telling you, Dawg. She tricked me. We talked about it. I had no idea she even knew Kelly. And honestly, I really didn't expect you to agree to that shit in the first place, but when you did, I was like, let's see what happens," Bill said. "Then when we watched them move around on the GPS tracker, I thought you were into it."

"A GPS tracker?" Leela repeated. She wanted to gouge Riley's eyes out with her fingernails.

Malone eased next to Leela. He reached for and touched her arm. "I need to explain."

She jerked beyond his touch and moved away from him. In a crowded room, she had never felt so alone. She didn't know who was telling the truth and chances of her being able to trust anyone seemed to shrink with each word spoken.

"I don't have anything else to say to you."

"Sweetness. This may have started out wrong, but think about it. Think about what we feel for each other. We don't have to throw it all away. You said yourself, he doesn't respect you; he talks down to you; acts like you're a kid. It's obvious, he's forgotten what he had in you."

With narrowed eyes, Leela turned to Malone and said, "But you've been playing out some twisted fantasy all along. What was the prize for you? What would've labeled you a winner? When were you gonna be done with me and on to your next assignment?"

"Sweetness, it's not like that. Natasha wasn't up front when she approached us. She made it seem like it was friends hooking up. I swear to you, she never said all of this was because she wanted your husband."

Malone's voice begged and pleaded.

"Let her have him, Baby. I've got you. I swear, nothing has changed; I've got you."

"Dude. That's still my wife. I need you to step off," Riley said as he approached Malone. He turned to his wife."Leela, get your shit together, and let's bounce. We'll talk about this at home. I'm tired of this mess."

All eyes fell on Riley.

Leela was stunned that at this very moment, in light of all that had been revealed, he still carried on like he was in control. She didn't move an inch.

For the longest, Samantha and Kent stood back and watched in silence. She turned to him and asked, "So, the only reason you're with me is because you were helping her out?"

"Nah. She did approach us, but she made it seem like we were all going to hook up. All she did was put us in the same place at the same time, like a blind date. I don't know this chick like that," Kent quickly said. "That night we sent the drinks over, she was there and told us some story about how you two were her friends. She had to leave, but was concerned about you guys having a good time. That was it. She pointed you and Leela out, and Malone and I took it from there. This is no conspiracy. If she did anything more than that, she did that shit all on her own."

Samantha looked at Bill. "So you sold your friend out for what? Some ass? You're a real piece of work."

"I didn't sell anybody out for nothing. Natasha has a way of appealing to what people want most. She's right. I wanted my friend to remember the good ol' days. That's all I'm guilty of. I might have helped her a little more than I should have, but don't try to make this out to be nothing more than what it was," Bill warned.

Samantha was disgusted. She rushed to Leela's side. "What do you want to do? You don't have to go with him if you don't want to. I can make everyone leave, and we can try to figure this thing out. Just tell me what you want to do."

Riley stepped up. "What the hell do you mean what does she want to do? Last I checked, I still had papers on her! That's my damn wife. She's gonna do what the hell I tell her to do," he stated.

Natasha stepped into Riley's personal space. She spoke to him calmly, as if no one else was in the room.

"See, Baby. That's what I'm trying to tell you. This type of woman will never appreciate you. Women no longer want a real man like you. They don't want a man who is going to take control of a situation and tell them what to do. They're too busy trying to compete with men. But me, I'm different. If you were my husband, you would never have to raise your voice. You say it's time to go, and, Baby, I'm going. You're too good of a man to have to repeat yourself the way you do. Don't you get that? Let me treat you like the king you are." Natasha moved close to Riley.

When he didn't back away, Leela wondered if what she'd heard was correct. There was nothing appealing to her about Riley's demanding ways and condescending tone. The fact that Natasha found it attractive made her feel like the disturbed woman might have had a point.

CHAPTER 37

Leela struggled to steady her breathing. She was so enraged she felt like she could kill. She motioned for Samantha to come close, and when her friend came, she reached in and whispered, "Make them go, all of them."

"You got it!"

Samantha walked into the center of the small crowd that had formed in her living room. She clapped her hands a few times to get everyone's attention.

"Okay, listen here, everyone. It's time to go. This entire mess is over. We're tired of it and we need you all to leave."

Riley frowned and looked at Leela with such disgust and disdain she knew his mind probably raced with the many ways he could kill her. "Leela, c'mon. Let's go!"

Silence fell on the room once again. All eyes focused on Leela, including Riley's.

"Look, I've had enough of this circus. Let's get outta here and go home," he repeated. "We can straighten this out in private."

"I'm not going," Leela said. At first her voice wasn't that loud. The tension in the room was similar to a foggy day with zero visibility.

Riley moved closer. When Leela flinched, Malone quickly jumped between them.

"Man, she says she ain't going," Malone said. "And I don't think anybody in here is about to let you force her to go."

"Dude, who the hell do you think you talking to? This is my wife! I don't care what you think you got with her; she belongs to me!" Riley growled.

"Riley, that's where you're wrong. I don't belong to you! At this point, I don't even know that I wanna still be married to you! I'm not leaving and that's that!"

"You're making a huge mistake," Riley said. His voice was laced with anger.

"I'll take my chances, but I'm staying right here."

Natasha moved in and gently took Riley by the arm. "You don't have to take this. Let her stay if that's what she wants to do, Daddy. I'll come with you, and you never gotta worry about begging me."

"Begging?" Riley gawked. "I ain't begging nobody for shit!"

"I know. I know. That's what I'm trying to say. Let's get out of here. Let's leave them all here to figure this out. She wants to stay; let her. You're too much of a man to have to persuade any woman to go with you."

Natasha turned her head and allowed her eyes to stare at Leela's feet. The frosty, defiant stare slowly rolled up to her head, stopped at her eyes, where they lingered for a second, then plummeted back down, again. "You're too good for her anyway," Natasha snarled.

Riley stared at his wife too. He didn't say anything, but he was sure she understood, despite his silence.

"Babe." Natasha stepped up to Riley and moved into his personal space. She rubbed his arm. "You don't need this. I'm embarrassed for you. I don't understand how you're allowing things to go down like this. Baby, let's go!"

Riley's icy glare connected with Natasha's eager eyes. She pleaded with him silently again, then slowly shook her head. Riley gently removed her hand and nodded.

"You're right," he said. His voice was so low, Natasha was probably the only person who heard it.

Kent was visibly upset too.

Before he left, Kent turned to Samantha. "Baby, I'm leaving now, but I won't stay away. I'm gonna respect your wishes, but I'm gonna call and check on you guys later." Kent turned to Malone. "Let's roll, Man."

Malone refused to leave. "I'm not going until he leaves, without her." He motioned toward Riley.

Once again, Riley's face filled with rage. He was still reluctant to leave, but Samantha and Natasha were both pushing him to go.

At the front door, Natasha gave his arm another tug, before they finally walked out of the door. Once they were gone, Malone followed behind Kent and finally, Leela and Samantha were left alone.

"What the fuck just happened here?" Samantha asked. "What the hell?"

Nearly two hours after the drama unfolded, Leela and Samantha got comfy on the couch, sipped cocktails, and talked about the details of the crazy evening.

It was so hard to fathom all that had gone down.

"Can you believe Natasha was behind all of this? She wanted him that bad?"

Leela turned to Samantha. "Does it matter to you that she basically set Bill up? I mean, the whole thing with Kelly."

"Bill is just as dumb as a box of rocks! It doesn't matter because as crazy as she is, she had a great point. If things were stable with Bill and me, Kelly wouldn't have had a chance. He's weak-minded. Think about it: how you gonna let this crazy chick talk you into getting your boy to do something like that in the first damn place?" Samantha asked. "Then the whole GPS thing? What the hell? So Free Fridays was a ploy from the gate!"

"Well, it's like ol' girl said; he wanted his friend to be single, just like him." Leela sighed.

"When a woman is desperate, um, I mean, determined, I guess there's no telling what she will do," Samantha said. She shook her head.

"So, that trick was probably following us all along," Leela said. "Think about it. How did she know we would be at that bar? And did she just pick two random guys when she found Kent and Malone? She was serious about hers, huh?"

"Well, we've known she was crazy from way back in the day. Obviously, she never took her meds or wherever she went, things didn't work there, so she came back to get her man!"

Leela held up her cocktail glass. "Let's toast to desperate, um, I mean, determined women who get exactly what they want!"

"Hell, I'll drink to that." Samantha raised her glass too. After they touched glasses, and took healthy sips, they laughed at the madness of it all.

"Malone was right about everything he said. There's no reason why I need to stay with Riley. I've put up with his shit for far too long. And besides, I'm not about to be stalked by that crazy bitch. Desperate or determined, if she went through all of this, you know good and well, she's not gonna stop until she gets his ass!"

"You gotta love 'em, those determined women," Samantha joked.

Her cell phone rang.

"Oooh. That's Kent, I'm not sure what to make of him. How do we know he's not more connected to Natasha than they're saying? I don't know."

Samantha picked up the phone and slid her finger across the

screen to decline the call. A few seconds later, the phone chirped and an indicator popped up to say she had a voicemail message.

"Umph. He left a message." She punched the necessary keys and listened.

"Baby, I hope you two are okay over there. I know there's a lot of confusion going on, but you gotta believe me when I tell you—that girl, Natasha, she don't mean shit to me. I swear I just met her that night. I wouldn't lie to you. Real talk, Baby, what we got going right now is real cool and I don't wanna see it messed up over some meaningless woman. I'm not gonna press, but I ain't backing down, either. That's it for now."

"Yeah, we need to talk about this," Samantha said after she listened to the message. "I ain't trying to be nobody's fool, but honestly, I kinda believe him."

Leela didn't miss the twinkle in Samantha's eyes. There was a part of her that wanted to believe what the guys were saying. The way Malone touched her, she didn't want to believe he was in cahoots with anyone. There was something so sincere and trustworthy about him, his kiss.

"If Natasha knew them…" Samantha said.

Leela finally interrupted. "I hope you don't mind, but right now, I don't know who or what to believe. My heart is telling me that Malone is the real thing, but after being with Riley and seeing how he operates, I'm so confused."

Samantha got up and moved to be near Leela.

"Will we ever get past this?" Leela asked. "I'm so tired of being caught between two men. I want stability back in my life again. I want to be able to have faith in the man I'm with." Leela sighed. "I know how you feel about marriage and men now, but I know you're not trying to be alone, are you?"

"No, not at all. I just want to clear this mess up."

CHAPTER 38

A few days later, still at Samantha's house, Leela stared deeply into the dark eyes that had completely held her captive. She felt so at ease despite the turmoil that had suddenly become her life. There was something so calming and reassuring about him.

"I'm sorry for all of this, Sweetness; the last thing I ever wanted to do was hurt you. If we had the slightest inkling that ol' girl was trying to target you and Samantha, there was no way in hell we would've played along. You know me well enough to know that's not my style. I'm sorry for all of it."

"This is a mess, isn't it?"

"It doesn't have to be. I mean, I get it. I know he's still your husband and you will have to go back there, but I can make sure you're safe. I won't let anything happen to you." He put up his two fingers. "Scout's honor, Sweetness."

Leela shook her head. "That's not a concern. Riley isn't violent; he's way too proud to go out like that. Besides, if he's with Natasha, there's no way in the world he wants to make himself look weak. That's just how he is."

Malone took her hands into his. He stroked her softly. "Well, regardless of what happens, I meant it when I said I got you." He took her chin and turned her face to his. Malone's mouth covered hers. Their kiss was intense, just the way Leela liked it. Everything with him, and about him, felt so right to Leela.

She wanted desperately to stay right there in Samantha's spare bedroom and in Malone's arms. She knew for sure she'd be safe if she could.

The knock on the door interrupted their tender moment.

"I'll get it this time," Leela said. "The last time you answered a door, I was not prepared for everything that flooded inside."

He laughed. "Good point."

Leela pulled the bedroom door open.

"Hey, I just wanted to let you know Kent brought food. You guys should get something to eat. It's good too, barbecue."

"You hungry?" Leela looked over her shoulder at Malone.

"Yeah, but not just for food."

"Behave!" Leela warned.

"What? I'm only being honest."

Sixteen months later…

Two years ago, if someone would've told Leela that she and Riley would be living separate lives and acting as if they barely knew each other, she would've called the person deranged.

But there she sat, hundreds of miles away from him and the life they once shared, marveling at just how much her life had changed over the course of two short years. She knew the change was for the best, because during that time, she had been the happiest in her life.

"It's so peaceful here," Samantha said.

The comment pulled Leela back from her thoughts. She sat gazing out of the patio door into the azure Caribbean Sea.

From her room that overlooked the sandy white beach, she focused on two palm trees that were decorated with white ribbons, colorful flowers and streamers that seemed to dance in the wind.

With the bright blue skies as a backdrop, the image was near perfect.

"I love it here," Samantha said.

"Talk about paradise," Leela said.

They were inside a deluxe suite at Robert's Grove Beach Resort in Placencia, Belize.

"It's peaceful and beautiful here, isn't it?" Leela asked.

"It is. Can you believe it? Everything is perfect. Almost too perfect if you ask me," Samantha said.

Leela turned to look at her friend. "We deserve a little perfection, my friend. Don't you think? But now that it's all over, everything worked out the way it should've for us all."

Samantha walked closer to Leela. They both looked out at the scene that seemed to sprawl out before them.

"I'm so happy for you. The past few days here have been the closest I've ever been to paradise," Samantha said. "You made yet another great choice."

"How do I look? You know I didn't know how I'd feel in this color, but I'm glad I didn't go with white. That's not the kind of marriage I want, not again." Leela fussed with the dress a little.

"You look perfect. Here, wait, let me get one last thing; then I think we need to get going."

Samantha left Leela's side and rushed to the nightstand. She grabbed a small plastic container, removed the colorful flower and approached Leela.

"Here, turn your head to the left," Samantha said. Carefully, she pinned the flower to the side of her best friend's hair and stepped back to survey her work. "There, that's perfect. You look great."

"You look great, too."

"Thanks, girl. Now, let's go. We don't wanna keep our guests waiting, do we?"

Samantha moved around the room and picked up a few items.

"We can go, but before we go down, let's stop next door. I need to check something," Leela said.

"Oh, girl, I told you, you look great!" Samantha assured her. "Hell, you were ready before me. What did you forget?"

"No, it's not that. I just need to make sure they put something in our room for later."

They left Samantha's room and walked a few feet down the hall. Leela pulled the key from the small satin wristlet she wore, and opened the door. She stuck her head inside and glanced around the spacious room.

"Yup, it's there," she said.

Once she eyed the standing silver bucket that held a bottle of champagne and saw the platter covered with strawberries, she pulled the door shut and grabbed Samantha by the arm. Leela was excited and couldn't wait for them to return to the room later.

"Can you believe this?" Leela asked as she walked next to Samantha. "I am really about to do this, huh?"

"You bet your ass you are!" Samantha exclaimed.

As they walked through the halls and along the grounds of the resort, employees and guests stopped to gaze at them. The women were both all smiles and beamed as they moved past the bar on the wooden deck and beyond the pool.

Moments later, Leela and Samantha arrived at the area that was cordoned off, and everyone rose. The women smiled as oohs and ahhs rose from the people arranged in chairs on the beach front.

When the soft music started, they each took the stroll down the aisle and toward the groom and his best man who waited at the makeshift altar.

The destination wedding was intimate and small, with twenty guests; it was exactly what the bride and groom wanted. After the ceremony wrapped up, guests at the resort and nearby resorts were treated to a reception party in the open restaurant.

Leela was finally happy. She and her husband held hands throughout the entire evening. After they partied with their guests, Malone leaned to whisper in his wife's ear. "Sweetness, let's go back to our room."

Leela smiled and they slipped away from the party. At the door, Leela dug into the satin wristlet for the key, and pulled it out, but Malone stopped her. He took the key, unlocked the door, then scooped her up into his arms and carried her over the threshold.

Leela giggled the entire time. She felt incredible. She was in love and was married to a man who was good to her. Leela wanted to remember the way she felt on her wedding day so she could mentally revisit their time in Placencia whenever she needed. Inside the suite, they fed each other sweet strawberries that they washed down with ice-cold champagne.

"I love you, Sweetness," Malone said.

"I love you more," Leela replied.

Back in Houston, Natasha had prepared a special day for her man and herself. She knew Leela's wedding day would be a challenge for Riley, but she planned to keep him busy and keep his mind off any thoughts of that woman.

Who jumps right into another marriage before the ink dries on the divorce papers? It was shameful to her, but she was glad Leela was stupid. That meant Natasha wouldn't have to worry about the ditz trying to get back with her man.

It had taken lots of work and patience on her part, but she knew she was right when she found the right man for Leela. It took some time for Riley to realize it, but Natasha knew he would eventually, and she waited patiently.

"Your breakfast is ready, Baby," she cooed.

She waited on Riley like an obedient servant, and she was happy to do it. Due to smart investments from a small inheritance she'd received when her great-aunt died, Natasha only worked a part-time job, so the bulk of her time was devoted to taking care of Riley's needs.

The night they left Samantha's house nearly two years ago, Riley seemed determined to hold on to his wife and that pathetic marriage.

"Listen, I can drop you wherever you need to go," Riley had said.

"I wanna go with you. Don't you get it? I'm your ride-or-die. I don't want you to be alone tonight. You've been through so much already."

Riley had looked over at her. For a long time, he didn't say anything.

"Why did you go through all of this? What is it about me?"

"I told you. Men like you really don't exist anymore. I don't see you as a threat. I love your Alpha-male characteristics. I think if more men took control, the way you do, this world would be a better place."

"It ain't easy to deal with me," Riley had warned. "Some people would even call me an asshole. I told you before, Natasha, you don't want this work."

"I'm not looking for anything easy. I think I have shown you that I'm prepared to work hard for everything I want. I don't shy away from hard work. I wanted you, and I put everything on the line to get you. I took a gamble. For all I knew, Bill could've ignored Kelly's advances and this whole thing would've blown up in my face," she said.

"How'd you know it would work?"

"Like I said before, you're not like most men. Bill is weak. Nothing against him, but if he was half the man you are, there was no way I would've been able to make it work. But because he's weak, I knew he'd be no match for Kelly. She was glad to help. We met and she told me all of her business; that's when I knew she'd be perfect. It was nothing but a game for her."

"But what have you been doing all this time? It took a minute for it to all work out," Riley said.

"I've been taking care of myself, keeping my body tight, working my business, and focusing on the ultimate prize."

He simply nodded and drove the rest of the way to his house. Once they arrived, Natasha got out and followed him inside. She'd been by his side ever since.

"You're a good woman, Natasha," Riley said.

In their time together, he still hadn't said he loved her, but she knew he did. If he didn't, she felt like he could grow to love her, eventually. It didn't matter. She had enough love for them both and as long as he respected her and was honest, she felt they had a real chance.

"I feel like doing something later, but I'm not sure what," Riley said as he finished the food she had prepared.

Before he could move from the table, Natasha was up and clearing the dirty dishes. She rinsed everything and loaded them into the dishwasher.

"You can go and relax and I'll think of something for us to do. Don't stress yourself, Honey. I can come up with something we'll both enjoy."

Riley looked at her before he walked out of the kitchen.

She never asked about his thoughts; she was just glad to be a part of his life. Natasha did everything she thought he might like, and when she was off the mark, she asked him to tell her what he wanted.

Natasha was confident that he would come around; she had already staked quite a bit on that belief.

Bill regretted everything he had done to his best friend, and he hated what it had cost him. Life without Riley was boring and predictable.

Since Riley and Natasha started living together, the phone calls became fewer and fewer, until one day, they simply stopped. In order to get his job back, he had to agree to a transfer, and had been moved to the company's new start-up in Sugar Land.

That meant he was farther away from Riley and that made the gap between them widen even more.

He had heard about the wedding, but there was no way in hell he was going. He didn't care what Linda said. They'd been kicking it on the low for a few months and to his surprise, things were going pretty well.

She wasn't the nicest woman, and she could be pushy at times, but Bill told himself she was something to do.

"You missed a beautiful ceremony," Linda said, when she called.

"Aw, all that crap is for women anyway. Don't be out there and find yourself some young island man," Bill joked. "Sounds to me like someone might be a little worried," she teased.

"Nah. It's all good. I just know how you feel about younger men, that's all."

Once he ended his call with Linda, Bill tried to figure out what he could get into for the night. He didn't really go out much anymore and most of his time was focused on work.

Although he didn't want to broadcast his association with Linda to the world, he felt comfortable kicking it with her.

Because she was older, he didn't have to worry about some of the childish shit younger chicks did. She had her own money, so she wasn't in his pockets.

After one good round of sex, she'd smoke a cigarette and drift off to sleep. She wasn't trying to break his back or get him to do all kinds of freaky shit that he'd had enough of.

The only issue he had was the constant nightmares that woke him up in cold sweats. In one, he was surrounded by Leela, Samantha, her new husband, Riley, Linda's mother and father, and Linda, when Natasha burst into the room and screamed at him about being weak.

Right there in front of everyone, he'd cower down and beg her to leave him alone. He felt like she was the true source of all the loss he'd recently experienced.

But Bill wasn't the type to verbalize any of that to anyone. Instead, he went about his daily routine and got with Linda maybe once or twice a week.

When he looked back on everything that had happened, he told himself it was all for a good reason. He just didn't know what that reasoning was, and he resigned himself to the fact that he might never find out.

Bill took a beer, sat in front of the TV and started to surf the channels. He watched the game, until the game watched him; then he retired to bed.

It wasn't the most exciting life, but it was his and it was what he had. Besides, Linda would be back by Monday and he'd drop in on her for a day or two. He finally realized that the good ol' days were gone for good.

READER'S DISCUSSION GUIDE

1. What did you think about each character's personality?

2. Why did Riley think his wife needed him to control her?

3. Why was Leela so impacted by what happened to Samantha's marriage to Bill?

4. Is a friendship able to survive divorce among friends?

5. What should Leela's grandmother have done differently when she learned about her husband's betrayal?

6. Do you think Linda's reaction to the betrayal was valid?

7. Why was Leela so easily lured away from her marriage to Riley?

8. Was Natasha brilliant or desperate?

9. What's a deal breaker for marriage?

10. Should marriage evolve with changing times?

11. Are all divorces a sign of failure?

12. Were Samantha's new views on marriage understandable?

13. Where would you like to see these characters in five years?

14. Did Leela jump back into a relationship too soon?

15. Can Riley and Natasha make it?

ABOUT THE AUTHOR

By day, Pat Tucker works as a radio news director in Houston, Texas. By night, she is a talented writer with a knack for telling page-turning stories. A former TV news reporter, she draws on her background to craft stories readers will love. She is the author of seven novels and has participated in three anthologies, including *New York Times* bestselling author Zane's *Caramel Flava.* A graduate of San Jose State University, Pat is a member of the National and Houston Associations of Black Journalists and Sigma Gamma Rho Sorority, Inc. She is married with two children.